the LAST BLACK CAT

ALSO BY

Eugene Trivizas

The Three Little Wolves and the Big Bad Pig
Illustrated by Helen Oxenbury

The LAST BLACK CAT

Eugene Trivizas

Translated by Sandy Zervas

EGMONT

To my cat,
Agatoula

EGMONT
We bring stories to life

First published in Great Britain 2005
by Egmont Books Limited
239 Kensington High Street
London W8 6SA

First published in Greece 2001

Original Greek text copyright © 2001 Eugene Trivizas
English language text copyright © 2005 Sandy Zervas
Illustration copyright © 2005 Jessica Meserve

The moral rights of the author, translator and
illustrator have been asserted

ISBN 1 4052 1281 0

1 3 5 7 9 10 8 6 4 2

A CIP catalogue record for this title is available from the British Library

Typeset by Avon DataSet Ltd, Bidford on Avon, Warwickshire
Printed and bound in Great Britain
by Cox & Wyman Ltd, Reading, Berkshire

Contents

I'm telling you this story,
because here, on our island,
like anywhere else,
cats forget,
people forget,
and it won't take much
for the madness
to begin all over again . . .

1

The raid on the fish tavern

In which, following a series of mysterious and inexplicable feline disappearances, our hero witnesses a cat-napping and sees the short man with the cap for the first time.

Silktail was the first to disappear. Then Springer. There followed Whiny, Giuseppe, Rameses, Soggy, Lothario and Bijou. All these cats had nothing in common except for one thing: their colour. Their inky black colour.

At first, these sudden vanishings didn't particularly worry the island's cat population. It isn't really that rare for a cat to make himself scarce on a whim. There could be millions of reasons for his disappearance: his owner might have moved to another neighbourhood, or some sour old housewife might have put him under lock and key to stop him roaming. Or it might just be that the cat has got it into his head to catch a sneaky mouse, and is laying siege to its hole day and night, patiently waiting for the mouse to show its muzzle so that he can pounce on it and turn it into the dish of the day.

Personally, I didn't lose any sleep over the matter until one fateful summer night.

That evening, you know, I was going to meet my best mate, Choptail, also known as Commandocat or the Sizzler, because of his prowess at sniffing out and snatching fried fish from seashore fish taverns and making off with them like a shot. A cool cat, Choptail – a real mate – always looking on the bright side, with a merry sparkle in his eye. Together we'd had some high old times, I can tell you. We hung around together, lolled about in the sun, prowled the rooftops and stuffed ourselves silly with grab-it-yourself meals whenever we had the opportunity.

At the crack of dawn earlier that day, Choptail had let on that during one of his afternoon prowls he had spotted a fish tavern by the sea with a kitchen window that wouldn't close properly. We had agreed to meet near there in the early evening to plan the strategic assault and honour the premises with a lightning raid that would empty the frying pans and fill our bellies.

Our meeting place was the tin roof of a rickety old shed, about three hundred metres from our target. As always on such operations, we had chosen a night with only a thin sliver of a moon, which drastically reduced the chance of our movements being detected. An elementary precaution you would say, but one we had learned the hard way, as past raids on fish taverns and similar charitable establishments during a full moon had cost us dear.

To cut a long story short, I arrive first, shoot up a rusty drainpipe and start pacing up and down on the roof. I feel cheerful and carefree, on top of the world. The view is marvellous from up here. On my right, the sea stretches away, dark green and infinite, as far as the eye can see. Years ago, when I was young, just a teensy weensy kitten, in fact, I used to dream that one day I would become a ship's cat, board a five-masted clipper laden with crates full of sea bream and monster lobster and sail the seven seas.

I'd savour exotic moonfish and king crab in tropical ports, I'd climb fishbone trees in fairytale jungles and have torrid love affairs with passionate kitties in Siam, Afghanistan and Persia.

But alas! My dream remained but a dream – I get seasick, you see. Tonight, though, the sea is calm, smooth like olive oil before you put it in a pan to fry bonito, and the pale reflection of the stars glimmers on its mirror-like surface. But in winter, god Bastet almighty! How this same sea can change! It seethes and rages, angry waves rise up like huge mountains, one hurricane follows another and, for three or four months, neither ship, caique nor any other vessel can approach our island.

Anyway, as I was saying, I'm checking out what is going on from up here on the roof. A bit further down, to my right,

I can clearly see the whitewashed walls of the fish tavern – The Jolly Shrimp – and, through the lighted kitchen window, the shadow of the cook, ol' Mr Anestis, who's scrubbing his frying pans in blissful ignorance of our plans, wiping the sweat off his brow with the corner of his apron. There are hardly any customers at the wooden tables with faded red and white checked tablecloths by the sea – just an old captain with his parrot and two pairs of lovebirds holding hands. The distant sound of their voices reaches my ears and the mouthwatering aroma of frying mullet teases my nostrils.

My belly rumbles impatiently but I reassure it, vowing that I will soon make it happy. Not that this reassurance has the desired effect – my tummy rarely trusts me because my culinary promises have more often than not remained unfulfilled.

Suddenly, the unexpected happens. A black tomcat whom I've never seen before emerges from under an upturned fishing boat, apparently drawn by the enticing, irresistible smell of the mullet.

Here we go! I hope the idiot doesn't ruin it for us! I think to myself. I watch him as he cautiously draws nearer the fish tavern, casting furtive glances all around him.

The rest happens so suddenly, that I later found myself wondering whether I had really witnessed it or not. A motorbike with a sidecar roars full throttle up the road and comes to a sudden, screeching halt. Two blokes – a short one wearing a greasy cloth cap and a tall one with a droopy moustache – jump off, deftly scoop the cat up in a shrimp net, kick him in the ribs and bundle him into a sack. The wretched cat starts squirming, trying to claw his way out, mewing desperately, but to no avail. The kidnappers throw their victim into the sidecar, hop back on to the motorbike again and speed off into the night.

I can't believe my eyes. Paralysed with shock, I waste precious time as I'm not quite sure how to react. Should I wait for my buddy, Choptail, as we'd agreed, or should I run after the villains? On the one hand, there's my hungry belly, on the other, a fellow feline in desperate need. I hesitate for a moment or two, but then I quickly make up my mind. With an almighty leap, I land in the road and start chasing after them as fast as I can. It's no use. Try as I might, the motorbike is faster than I am and soon it disappears into the dark end of the street.

Out of breath, I start back. As I am passing the spot where the kidnappers struck, with my tail hanging down, a shiny metallic object on the asphalt catches my eye. By the look of it, the villains must have dropped it. I approach, I turn it over with my front paw, sniff it and examine it carefully. It's a pin, the kind people sometimes wear on their lapels. It's a silver horseshoe enclosing a four-leafed clover picked out in green enamel. Odd. What could it possibly mean?

I don't have time to think about it properly. A sudden honk frightens me out of my skin and a monstrous twelve-wheel lorry roars past, missing me by a whisker. It's a miracle I'm not squashed flat! I return double quick to my rendezvous point and climb to the roof of the shack to find an uneasy Choptail, who is waiting for me, a trifle irritated.

'Hey, dude! Where were you? Didn't we say we'd see about fish today? What's up? I've been worried about you. Where have you been?'

'Get a load of this, Choptail! Two blokes, a short one with a greasy cloth cap and a tall one with a droopy moustache, bundled a cat into a sack.'

'You don't say! Really? What kind of cat?'

'A black one, like us!'

'And what's it to you?'

'Come on, Choptail! If you were in his place, wouldn't you want someone to care what happened to you? And on top of everything, they beat him up! Who knows where they've taken the poor bleeder . . .'

'You're right!' Choptail admitted. 'But what can we do? Now you come to mention it, there's something fishy going on in our crowd these days. Hardly a day goes by without a cat disappearing! Do you think those two blokes you saw have got something to do with the rest of the vanishings? I mean, there's Silktail and Springer, Whiny and Giuseppe, Rameses, Soggy, Lothario and Bijou.'

'There's only one way to find out.'

'What do you mean?'

'We should track down the two villains.'

'How?'

'By the smell. One of them, the short one with the greasy cap, has a distinctive scent.'

'What kind of scent?'

'He smells of iodine and mint.'

'Yeah, right. That's a great help. Yikes! What's that noise? A tractor going by?'

'Don't be stupid! And stop exaggerating! It's my tummy protesting!'

'There you go! We start gabbing and forget the most vital matter of all! Grub. The fish tavern will be closing any minute now and we'll miss our chance. Are you ready?'

'Ready to go and all set! Have you worked out how to pull it off?'

'Of course. Are you listening?'

'With absolute concentration.'

'Well then. I shall create a diversion. You see the captain who's sitting at that table over there? I'll pounce on his parrot. As soon as the cook comes out to see what's going on, you snatch a fish and when he starts chasing you, I'll grab whatever I can.'

'Purrfect!'

Our raid on the fish went like clockwork. The diversion worked a treat; we grabbed a mullet each from the frying pan and made short work of them.

Afterwards, to help us digest, we strolled light-heartedly along the beach, at a safe distance, of course, from the fish tavern. We gazed at the stars' reflection in the water. We listened to the sea that flowed noiselessly between the rocks and ebbed with a sweet gurgling sound. I was lost in pleasant thoughts.

Choptail was in high spirits and struck up his favourite song, 'Abigail with the lovely tail':

> *I knew a cat called Abigail*
> *Who had such a lovely tail*
>
> *All the tom cats stood in line*
> *To date this divine feline.*
> *They got the deepest thrill*
> *From her tail's dainty frill.*
>
> *There they lay*
> *To see it sway*
>
> *You are pretty,*
> *Little kitty,*
> *So I sing this little ditty*
>
> *Ah, I wish, my sweet Abigail*
> *You had more than just one tail!*
> *It would be tremendous fun*
> *If you had twelve tails instead of one.*

'What do you say to a second course?' Choptail enquired after a while. 'The cook will still be exhausted with all this running. He won't be able to chase us all over again. Didn't you see him? He was huffing and puffing like a steam engine going up the hill.'

'It would be nice, but I'll have to take a rain check.'

'Why? Don't tell me you're full?'

'Nope, I've got a date.'

'With Graziella?'

'Who else?'

'Graziella, always Graziella.'

'She's been waiting for me! It wouldn't be right to disappoint her.'

'You lucky devil,' said Choptail, admiringly. 'I don't know what she sees in you but she's stuck on you like a sardine in a tin.'

'Nor do I, but so long as she is, I have no intention of removing her.'

And with these words, I bade Choptail adieu and took the road that would lead me to Graziella's velvety embrace.

2

Cuddles and Graziella

In which two cats exchange vows of undying love, before a surly bulldog interrupts their romance.

Graziella was a fabulously beautiful Angora cat I'd met in a rather odd way, thanks to a mouse called Cheapskate. While chasing this rodent, I had found myself at high noon in the garden of a luxurious residence and there I first laid eyes on her, stretched out like a goddess on a bed of red flowers, washing herself with her little rosebud of a tongue. What a dream! What a divine cat she was! What eyes! What velvety, snowy fur! What a fluffy tail! I fell head over paws in love. For this, I owed Cheapskate a debt of eternal gratitude, and not only had I stopped chasing him but we had become good mates.

Cheapskate lived in a mousehole in the house of a poet by the name of Peter Pentameter, the owner of an impressive, if very dusty, library whose shelves were crammed with poetic anthologies. Every now and then, my mate Cheapskate would come across romantic couplets in these anthologies.

He would adapt them suitably and then repeat them to me so that I could memorise them and whisper them into Graziella's adorable little ear. She loved listening to my little recitations.

Anyway, I arrive at the villa where Graziella lives, a really posh mansion smothered in pomegranate trees and oleanders, guarded by a grouchy old bulldog with an ugly mug, called Cuddles. Why anyone would call such a repulsive, blood-thirsty beast Cuddles, I never understood. Luckily, Cuddles was usually kept chained in his wooden kennel and we always took care to meet at a safe distance from him, near a goldfish pond in the shape of a six-pointed star.

When I get to our rendezvous, I meow soulfully. In other words, I give three long-drawn mews and two short and lusty ones. In a few minutes Graziella appears and descends lightly next to me on the marble paving round the star-shaped pond.

'You're late,' she complains.

'Just a tiny bit,' I say apologetically.

'You know how I have been longing to see you all day,' she purrs, flirtatiously.

'No, I don't. Tell me . . .'

'You tell me first.'

'Tell you what?'

'That you love me!'

'I love you,' I assure her.

'Louder! Meow out your love louder!'

'If I meow any louder, Cuddles will hear us.'

'If you really loved me, you wouldn't care about Cuddles.'

I feel honour-bound to do as she wishes. 'I looooooooove yoooooooooou,' I howl as loudly as I can.

What possessed me? I was asking for it. Before I knew where I was, the bulldog woke up, broke his chain and went for us.

We zoom up a bushy pomegranate tree. Cuddles parks himself underneath and barks as if someone is drilling holes in his tail. I pick a pomegranate and hurl it straight at his head. Cuddles realises that if he continues to lay siege to the tree, more missiles will follow and he returns to his kennel in a sulk.

'Will you love me forever?' asks Graziella with a purr.

'Longer. You?'

'And me. I shall love you as long as I live. I shall love you all my nine lives.'

When Graziella says that kind of thing it sends me to seventh heaven.

'My sweetheart! We'll have together nine whole lives of love!' I whisper affectionately, and I lick her snow-white ear.

'And the other one!' she purrs, blissfully.

I lick the other ear.

'Nibble it, just a little.'

I nibble it, just a little.

And then, drunk with the fragrances of the garden, we make mad, passionate love by the moonlight. The clumps of trees keep us out of sight from the house.

'You know something,' she says suddenly.

'What?'

'They are planning to have me mated.'

I was so surprised I nearly fell backwards into a flowerbed of daffodils. 'What did you say? Who are they going to mate you with?'

'With Rasmin.'

I'd never heard the name before. Nor could I imagine then the fatal role he would play in my life. 'Who is this Rasmin?'

'He belongs to Mrs Camilla Caprizioni, my mistress's childhood friend. He is an Angora cat too, you know.'

'So what if he's an Angora cat?' I say angrily. 'Does he have to drop his anchor in your port?'

'Our mistresses agreed on the match the other day, while they were having tea with lemon tart, petits fours, apple crumble and an angel cake with raisins and almond glazing.'

'I don't care what they were having for tea! Spare me the culinary details! Get to the point. What did they agree?'

'That we are suited. That we'd make the perfect couple.'

'Did they, now? Really? And how did the batty old cows come to this conclusion?'

'Don't be so rude about my mistress and her friend, if you please. It isn't nice. They came to this conclusion, as you put it, because we are the same breed and therefore our kittens will have perfect pedigrees.'

'Humph! And what about you? Didn't you tell them that you are going steady with someone else?'

'Even if I could do that, dear, they wouldn't care. Besides, you know humans. They could never understand that I had fallen in love with just a common alley cat.'

'Why? What's wrong with alley cats? They are fine, upstanding cats!'

'Especially you!'

'That's what I mean. Are those two women in their right minds? What business have they to meddle in your private life? Has Mrs Camilla Caprizioni nothing better to do than arrange marriages with every Tom, Dick and Harry?'

'You know something? I like it when you get angry. But there is no need. It's you I love . . .'

'Tell me,' I say casually. 'About this Rasputin . . .?'

'Rasmin!' she corrects me.

'Yeah, whatever . . . Rasmin. What's he like?'

'Handsome.'

'How handsome? Handsomer than me?'

'I don't love you because of your looks, my love!'

'Oh? Why do you love me then, "your highness"?'

'Because you're you!'

That's the kind of thing that Graziella says, and it sends me to cloud nine. But then, of course, she brings me back down. She has me going up and down as if I were a lift in a tower block.

But for the time being, at least, I was top cat in her eyes, and I swung my tail in relief.

'My pretty little pussy,' I croon, licking her dainty ear.

'Do you know something else?' she asks.

'What?'

'Next week, I am going to be in a cat beauty contest. You know, the shows that take place in the park with the lilac trees? The mayor will be there along with the deputy mayor, the ambassador of Purrsia and the rest of high society.'

'Why don't I escort you so we can win first prize as the most beautiful feline pair?'

'I'd rather you did not, if you don't mind! Come closer, now . . . Much closer!'

After a lot more love by moonlight, Graziella made forty vows and sixty-five promises that she would prefer a hundred thousand times to elope with me and live in the alleys, caring nothing for the north wind, the sleet, the rain and the rest of the elements, than to mate with Rasmin. She swore that if the arranged marriage went ahead, that's exactly what she intended to do.

But in spite of all these assurances, I confess that from that night on, I was consumed with curiosity to see what charms the great Rasmin had to offer.

3

The lovesick woodpecker

*In which three cats visit a three-star rubbish bin and
our hero helps a lovesick woodpecker return to its nest.*

The following morning, Choptail and I were enjoying
the warm morning sun, sprawled lazily on top of a
whitewashed wall that surrounded a garden with yellow
dahlias. We were joined by Purrcy, an unbelievably cuddly
cat whose weakness was to rub himself against the legs of
passers-by. He would follow them on a whim and start
weaving between their legs, begging for a tummy scratch.

'I've found a fan-cat-tastic three-star rubbish bin!' the
cuddle maniac informed us, brimming with joy.

For those who aren't in the know, we stray cats put
rubbish bins into categories, depending on their contents. A
rubbish bin full of tasty tidbits is awarded five stars. Rubbish
bins that contain slim pickings which are also well past their
consume-by date are awarded two stars at the most. As for
the catatonically sad rubbish bins that contain nothing but

sawdust, walnut shells and toilet paper, they fall into the minus-five-stars category.

On the other hand, one must admit that there are some fan-cat-tastic rubbish bins, like that of the chief justice, which we used to call 'the horn of plenty' because we could spend all night cleaning it up and always find it full to the brim with delicious snacks in the morning. The trouble was that all the cats on the island had got wind of it and you could hardly get a paw in for the crush. You had to be there very early, even before the crack of dawn, to be able to get a bite to eat. In the end, the chief justice, in an act of self-defence, was forced to hire two firemen to protect the coveted rubbish bin and hose down any cat who was foolhardy enough to get near it.

Choptail, Purrcy and I were on our way when a tiny little furball of a black kitten approached us.

'I've lost my mummy. Her name's Lara,' it said. 'Have you seen her anywhere?'

'No, but don't worry. You'll find her. She must be somewhere near,' we comforted it.

'She went to get me a little food and she disappeared. It's been three days now.'

'Listen, why don't you come with us and we'll rustle up something for you?' suggested Choptail, who had started to feel sorry for the poor little mite.

When we arrived at the three-star rubbish bin in the

backyard of a dairy shop, we were informed by some fellow diners that in the last days seven more cats had disappeared from the face of the earth. They were all black. One of them, in particular, who went by the name of Tarlulla of the Streets, was an old flame of mine. She was a very smart, squint-eyed cat who threw mice into total confusion, as they could never be certain where she was looking, so she caught them all the more easily.

'Well, fry my plaice in butter! Things are getting worse every day,' remarked Choptail, taking his face out of a pot of yoghurt.

'You couldn't have spoken a truer word. Whatever might have happened to all those cats?' Purrcy wondered.

I asked the kitten that had followed us to go and play for a while and then told Purrcy all about the nightmarish scene I had witnessed the previous night.

'Oh no!' said Purrcy, and licked a bit of yoghurt that was trickling down his muzzle. 'We've got to do something, guys!'

'You bet!' agreed all who were present.

'What, though?' asked Bumpy, a cat with a head covered in bumps from the boots the neighbours threw at him whenever he serenaded his feline charmers at night.

'Let us think about it,' said Choptail, and stirred the rubbish with his front paw hoping to unearth another yoghurt pot.

'A piece of advice for you, Purrcy,' I warned. 'If you

happen to run across a short man with a cap, who smells of iodine and mint, keep away! Don't even think of rubbing your head against him, you plonker, because he's bad news. Cuddles lead to troubles. Do you understand what I mean, Purrcy mate?'

'Don't you worry about me, guys! If I ever come across Shorty and his cap, I won't rub my head against him or ask for a tummy scratch. I'll restrain myself. I'll follow him and record all his moves in detail,' Purrcy assured us.

But that morning, to tell the truth, I was rather more preoccupied with the case of the handsome Rasmin than the incidents of the lost cats. I was dying to check him out. So, I decided to pay a surprise visit to Mrs Camilla Caprizioni's mansion to see for myself how handsome this much-advertised cat was. If I had the chance I'd challenge him to a duel and then I'd show him who was top cat in this neighbourhood.

I made up an excuse, said goodbye to Choptail, Purrcy, Bumpy and the rest of my fellow diners at the three-star rubbish bin, hit the road and took a shortcut through the gully.

Walking through the thick grass, bees buzzing in the brightly coloured flowers all around, I muttered vehemently to myself, 'Get a pawful of this, Rasmin! This one's for you, too! Pow! Here's one more as a wedding present!'

If he thought I was playing games he would be very much mistaken. I'd show him what a real alley cat can do!

Suddenly, as I'm walking, I hear the fluttering of wings. I freeze and scan the area with my expert eyes. Here it is! A wounded woodpecker with a broken wing is dragging itself among the reeds.

That's a nice little tidbit! I think and smack my lips.

Before he even knows I'm there, I surprise him with a well-executed jump and block his way. He makes an attempt to get away but it is hopeless. He's now looking at me with his little eyes full of panic and terror.

I stretch my front paw and step on his wing to immobilise him.

'Please, don't!' he tweets faintly.

'What did you say?'

'Don't hurt me! I'm – I'm –'

'What?'

'I'm . . . in love.'

Just like me! I think and suddenly I don't feel like eating him any more. Actually, I think I'm beginning to like him. 'What's your name?'

'Wallace,' the woodpecker chirps, out of breath.

I don't know why, but I can't help feeling sorry for the poor little beggar. 'How did you get your wing broken, then?'

'He hit me – with a sling.'

'Who did?'

'A boy with scabby knees.'

'The little scoundrel! Say, Wallace – where do you live?'

'At the wood with the lovesick woodpeckers.'

'Is that where your nest is?'

'Yes. On the walnut tree with the twelve hearts carved on its trunk.'

I don't know what came over me. Was it a benevolence crisis? A rush of unselfishness? A sudden attack of altruism? How should I know? Whatever it was, I decided to do a good deed before the malicious one I was intending to commit shortly.

'Don't you worry!' I said, withdrawing the paw that was pressing on to his wing. 'I'll take you home!'

So I carefully picked up Wallace in my mouth and carried him straight to the wood with the lovesick woodpeckers. The ground beneath the trees was studded with little blue and yellow flowers and the air was sweet with the intoxicating smell of lavender. The twitter of the birds drove you wild. All the trees had little hearts with initials carved on to their trunks.

Who would have ever thought that I'd rise to be a woodpecker ambulance one day? I climbed into a walnut tree with fresh, green foliage under Wallace's directions and lowered him carefully into his nest on a three-forked twig.

'I hope to be able to return your kindness one day,' he told me as I was leaving.

'No sweat,' I answered. 'Just consider yourself lucky that I had red mullet for dinner last night and lunch at a three-

star rubbish bin today so I'm not feeling particularly hungry.'

Then I bade him farewell and went straight to Mrs Camilla Caprizioni's mansion, hell-bent on settling my score with the handsome Rasmin once and for all.

4

The handsome Rasmin

*In which a handsome white tom cat gracefully accepts
the attentions of a chambermaid and a cat furdresser,
while two pairs of eyes observe the scene.*

At Mrs Camilla Caprizioni's mansion, I climbed on to the
ornate balustrade, wandered round the marble terraces
with the fluted columns, searched every flowerbed in the
garden, burrowed into the crystal-panelled greenhouses,
clambered on to bowers and pergolas, jumped from ledges to
balconies, yet there was no sign of Rasmin the magnificent. I
gave the premises the once-over one more time and behind
the glass panels of a sunroom, I saw a scene that, I must
admit, made me feel quite nauseous.

Amidst the exotic potted flowers that spanned the whole
range of the colours of the rainbow, there was a snow-white
tom cat, who was languidly tasting dainty delicacies off a
porcelain plate with the word 'Rasmin' painted on it in
delicate handwriting. I must say I was a tiny bit jealous. I'd

never had my dinner off such an exquisite little plate. Unless you count dustbin lids as plates or, should I say, serving platters.

As I watched behind the glass, a ginger-haired chambermaid, wearing a freshly ironed uniform and a starched bonnet entered the sunroom. She was carrying a glittering, light-blue satin cushion in her hands. Trailing behind her was an effete cat furdresser in an apricot-coloured waistcoat with mother-of-pearl buttons, a pair of linen trousers with an immaculate crease and a purple silk scarf tied loosely around his neck.

It wasn't long before Rasmin, reclining majestically on the blue cushion, started to receive the expert attentions of the cat furdresser, who used three different brushes to groom his coat, each of them fitted with a gold handle, if you please, while a phonograph with a crimson horn played a minuet, a few feet away.

'Do you like music?' someone meowed next to me.

'Not really. I prefer red mullets,' I replied.

I turned round and saw another cat and – whoa! – what a cat! As sweet as treacle, the saucy little minx! She had a slick black coat, a dainty tail and bright blue eyes. She wore a rose-coloured velvet ribbon round her neck with a little silver bell that sparkled in the sunlight. If I hadn't been in love with Graziella, that cat would have certainly interested me in many ways.

'Do you know His Nibs?' I asked, nodding in the direction of his Royal Highness who haughtily permitted the attentions of the cat furdresser.

'Yes!' the black cat sighed. 'Oh, yeeeessss!'

'What are you groaning for?' I asked, not a little miffed. 'Did you eat a stale fish head and get a sudden tummy ache?'

'Of course not, you fool! I love him!'

'Who? That lazy windbag?'

'He's not a lazy windbag and watch your mouth when you talk about Rasmin!'

'Well, if he's not a lazy windbag then, what is he? Eh? Eh? Tell me! What is he?'

'He's a charming cat and pretty as a picture . . . But, alas! I have no hope.'

'Why's that?'

'I've heard that his owners are planning to mate him with an Angora cat. Graziella . . . someone . . . Now what name is that, I ask you? Graziella! For crying out loud!'

'So that's the case, eh?' I tried hard to swallow as if something had got stuck in my throat.

'If only I had her here, in front of me that – that – Graziella, d'you know what I'd do to her? D'you know?'

'What?'

'I'd claw her eyes out!' snorted the black cat vehemently. 'I'd pluck her whiskers one by one with my bare paws!'

These were the exact sort of compliments I would have

secretly liked to pay to Rasmin myself and then tip a pan of hot spaghetti on his head, but I knew that if I ever tried to execute my plans I'd have my own whiskers plucked one by one by a dozen or so of his lackeys. And if there's something I hold sacrosanct and guard with my life, it is my precious whiskers.

'What's your name?' I asked the black cat, to whom I was taking all the more.

'Ebonina!'

'Say, Ebonina, where do you live, if I may so enquire?'

'Two blocks further down. At Lorenzo Latremore's.'

'Who's he when he's at home?'

'He's an opera tenor. Surely you must have heard of him.'

'No, thank God, I have not.'

Ebonina cast a contemptuous look at me. 'Whenever I can,' she went on, 'I slip out of the tenor's house to come and admire this divine feline.'

In the meantime, the cat furdresser had undone the bow from Rasmin's collar and was handing the ribbon to the ginger-haired chambermaid.

'Why is he giving her the ribbon?' I asked Ebonina, who, as I had gathered, was fully versed in everything that had to do with the cat of her dreams.

'So that she can wash it in rosewater and press it. Rasmin changes his ribbon daily, you know. They're all made of the finest Japanese silk!'

'You're kidding!'

'And on Sundays he wears a ribbon made of Venetian lace.'

'Really? Well, I never!'

Ebonina chose to ignore the irony in my voice. 'He's such a gorgeous cat,' she raptured. 'A purrfect prince! I imagine that he doesn't eat anything but lobster croquettes and boiled goldfish puree.'

I thought I might tell her a thing or two about loverboy and his diet but then I thought better of it and kept shtum. I cast a last glance at the sunroom. The cat furdresser was now spraying the divine feline with expensive perfume out of a blue crystal bottle, while the maid brought in a freshly ironed ribbon in a delicate shade of mauve.

I'd had enough. I said goodbye to Ebonina, who was glued to the spot, watching her idol with adoration, and headed towards the exit. As I was absent-mindedly walking past a bed of rosebushes, I stumbled upon a gardener with a big straw hat who was sprinkling the roses with rosewater from the silver bowl he held in his hands. I caught him by surprise and the bowl fell out of his hands. He swore at me under his breath and kicked me in the ribs with his thick, muddy boots. I was sure that had I been Rasmin, it would not have been a kick he sent in my direction, but a whole series of low bows and curtsies.

Anyway, what can you say? I left the opulent villa, walked down the avenue with the eucalyptus trees and started roaming aimlessly about the lanes, the closes and the crescents, while thinking that maybe the two of us – that is, Ebonina and myself – should work together to put a stop to Graziella and Rasmin's mating. Various cunning plans went through my mind in quick succession, each allowing me to dispose of Rasmin and keep my beloved Graziella all to myself, forever.

All of a sudden, something stopped me in my tracks, as if I'd been struck by lightning. It was that smell! That same smell! I recognised it immediately. Without pausing to think twice, without the slightest doubt, braving any danger, I decided to follow wherever it would lead me.

So I turn right. Then left. I flare my nostrils and sniff hard, two, three times just to make sure! There isn't the slightest doubt. Iodine and mint! Mint and iodine! The fatal smells! I hide in the opening of a door and check things out. A bit further down, outside a warehouse, next to a corner store, there's our mysterious friend! It's Shorty with the greasy cloth cap, all right. With the help of a tall bloke in a baggy sweater, he's loading a van with about a dozen wooden crates. It's an old van, battered and dented here and there, with dark red patches where it has been painted over.

Coming from within the crates I can hear what sounds like faint scratching and muffled meowing. I'm not quite sure, though. I could just be imagining things . . .

Puffing and blowing, the short man with the cap heaves

the last crate on to the van. He takes a little tin of mint drops out of his pocket, offers one to the young bloke with the baggy sweater and pops another into his mouth. I get a good look at his hands, his stubby fingers, his beefy arms. They're covered in sticking plaster and scratches that have been disinfected with iodine. I watch him climb on to the driver's seat, turn the ignition and step on the accelerator. My mind is in overdrive. What's in those crates? Is it what I think it is? Where's he taking them? What's he going to do with them? It's time for instant action.

I zoom up a eucalyptus tree and from there I execute a faultless vault and land silently on to the roof-rack of the van just as it zooms off in an unknown direction.

5

The Happy Oasis hamam

*In which our hero observes suspicious transactions in
the steam of a nightmarish hamam.*

We've been travelling for quite some time now, passing
places I've never seen before; desolate building plots,
roads full of potholes and run-down neighbourhoods with
children playing hopscotch and kicking balls made of cloth.
Finally, the van pulls up in front of an ancient-looking
building with a domed roof. On a peeling sign above the
front are the words, The Happy Oasis Hamam.

A few steps down the road there's a sleek open-top car with
its hood folded back and smart, cream leather upholstery.

The short man with the cap comes out of the van
and heads towards the building. I follow him. He unlocks
a door with cracked glass panels and a sign that reads,
Members Only. He enters and I just manage to squeeze in
behind him, fortunately without him being any the wiser.
As the door closes, one of the cracked glass panes collapses

and shatters to smithereens on the pavement.

The hamam is full of steam. The misty glass of the domed roof allows some hazy light to filter through. The floor and walls are covered in white tiles, most of them cracked. I can just make out some marble basins and alabaster benches. All of a sudden, the apparition of a man is silhouetted behind the thick steam; a tall, lanky man in a white suit and dark-green glasses. On his lapel he's wearing a pin identical to the one I spotted in the street near the fish tavern on the day of the raid.

'Have you got the stuff?' he says, in a husky voice.

'Sure,' answers Shorty and stuffs a mint drop into his mouth.

'How many?'

'Sixteen.'

'Black?'

'All of them.'

'Splendid!'

White Suit takes out a wallet made of white lizard-skin, counts eight crisp banknotes and hands them over to Shorty. 'Take care of them!'

'Won't you count them?'

'I trust you.'

'Fine.'

'What happened to your pin?'

'I must have dropped it somewhere.'

'Ask Barnaby to give you another one. I must be off now.'

'Are you going to the office?'

'Yes, I am. We've got a meeting of the Guardians.'

What sinister goings-on are taking place in this steam bath? I ask myself. Why have they brought the crates with the cats here? What are they planning to do with them? In what way are they going to 'take care' of them?

I decide to follow Shorty, who has already almost disappeared into the cloud of steam, but I have the rotten luck to step on a sliver of green soap, skid along the floor and, half-landing on my head, I let out a high-pitched squeal.

'What's this cat doing here?' says White Suit in a voice as snappy as a crocodile's jaws.

'Well, fry me in olive oil, I have no idea!'

'Take care of it! Give it the express treatment!'

'Yes, guv. Right away!'

With far too much zeal, Shorty lunges forward with a view to giving me the aforementioned treatment, but stepping on the same sliver of soap, he spins round a couple of times as if he's doing the Twist, which gives me the chance to manoeuvre myself out of there. I make a dash towards the exit, dart out of the broken glass pane on the door and then, executing a second, equally impressive jump, I land in the open-top car and bury myself under a raincoat that had been casually thrown on to the back seat.

Since I haven't managed to find out what Shorty is up to,

I am determined to see where the man in the white suit and dark-green glasses is going. What is this office he mentioned? What kind of guardians was he talking about? Who was he going to meet? And, most important, why did they want to 'take care' of me?

6

The Guardians of Good Luck

In which the members of a secret society hold a meeting and take important decisions without suspecting that a black cat is watching them.

As I lie hidden under the raincoat, I hear footsteps approaching. In case the man in white attempts to pick up or move his raincoat, I am prepared to lunge at him, give him a good, hard scratch and vanish on the spot. I don't need to put my plan into action, though. White Suit gets into the car and sits behind the steering wheel without detecting my presence. A second later, I hear the car engine rev up, the car shudders, the engine roars and off we go.

It's a long journey. On our way, we're temporarily held up by a postal-workers' demonstration and an ice-cream-van-operators' rally blocks our way at the crossroads – we've been having quite a few rallies and demonstrations on our island, lately. Half an hour later the car pulls up. The engine stops. I hear the driver's door open and then close again. I allow for one or two minutes before I dare poke my nose out, just in time to see White Suit go into a tall building further down the street.

I follow, hot on his heels, but once I'm through the entrance, White Suit is nowhere to be seen. Where has he gone? I wonder. Hell-bent on finding him, I climb up to the first floor. All the doors are closed, except for one that reads:

NATASHA BUCKOFFSKAYA
BALLET SCHOOL

Behind the half-open door, I can make out an elderly lady playing the piano and three little girls in white tutus who are dancing clumsily, missing their steps every now and then.

I decide to give Natasha Buckoffskaya's ballet school a miss, since the guy I'm after does not strike me as the type who's come here to perfect his pirouettes.

On the second floor there are two doors. One says:

LOST AND FOUND BUREAU

and the other:

RONALD RUNG
RIGGING LADDERS
IMPORTS/EXPORTS

Let's go further up. If I ever lose a rigging ladder, I know where to look for it. On the third floor I come across walnut wood-panelled double doors with highly polished fluted brass handles and a sign that says:

THE GUARDIANS OF GOOD LUCK
Please enter right foot forward

This is it. This must be the place. This is where the man went, and where I must go too. But the door is shut tight and there isn't even the tiniest gap between it and the floor. Well, there is one but I'd have to be paper-thin to squeeze my way through it.

I don't lose heart, though. Where there's a will, there's a way, as they say. Silently, I go up a few more floors, until I find an open skylight, then I pick up speed, jump on to a ledge and, exercising my unique and enviable climbing skills, I land on a half-moon-shaped balcony, leap on to the one next to it and find myself near a french window with heavy drapes. Luckily, they are not completely pulled back and I can sneak a careful look at the room inside. I was spot on. It *is* the office of the Guardians.

Hanging on the walls, in gilt frames, there are pictures of idyllic landscapes, covered in four-leafed clover. About ten grim men are sitting on high-backed chairs, round a table carved in the shape of a horseshoe. The youngest among them is barely thirty years old, the oldest is approaching seventy. About sixty-seven and a half, I'd say. They're all wearing the familiar pin of a light green four-leafed clover within a horseshoe. I prick up my ears.

'Brothers!' announces an elderly gentleman with grey, wavy hair and a blue bow tie, who I guess must be the Arch Guardian. 'I declare our meeting open.'

All eyes turn towards him.

'To begin with, I'd like to express to each one of you, my particular gratification with your laudable efforts in leading our campaign against bad luck to a successful conclusion. The ignorant call us superstitious; little do they know we are their saviours. I am confident that your devotion, perseverance, ingenuity and initiative will bring our difficult mission to an auspicious end and rid our island, once and for all, of the misfortune inflicted on us by none other than black cats. Our aim – may I kindly remind you – is to have wiped out all black cats from our island within a few months and certainly before the hurricane season sets in.'

The Guardians applaud politely. One is cleaning his glasses with a crisp white handkerchief. Another is loosening his tie.

What is the guy with the bow tie talking about? He's not all there! He must be barking mad! Lunatic Asylum – Enter Backwards, the sign on the door should read.

'Let's begin with a review of our activities so far,' the Arch Guardian continues, fondling a rabbit's foot he's taken out of his waistcoat pocket. 'What has the head of the Pursuit and Annihilation Squad got to say?'

The man in the white suit and the dark-green glasses clears his throat and begins to address the meeting.

'Our work is proceeding with the success anticipated. Yesterday we located and appropriately sorted out sixteen black cats. When added to those we took care of in the previous weeks, the total comes up to seventy-eight.'

A murmur of approval is heard.

'Splendid!'

'Bravo!'

'Brilliant!'

'Well done, sir!' the Arch Guardian smiles, straightening his blue bow tie.

'I'm also in the pleasant position to report that most of them were exterminated via the DH method.'

'Would you be so kind to remind me, if you please, what precisely the DH method is?' asks a Guardian with a thin, twisting moustache, wetting his fingers with spit before he uses them to give it extra curl.

'Why, it is the "drowning in a hamam" method. We

drown them in the bathtubs of a secluded hamam, which has been kindly donated to us by a distinguished member of our group.'

My knees have turned to jelly. My whiskers are a-quiver. My head is swimming. Lord almighty! They drown them! How's that possible? I must have misheard! My ears must be deceiving me!

'Besides the DH method, we also employ the PF method, that is the method of the poisoned fishbone; the SC method, that is the method of the spiky club; the EC method, which is the method of the explosive canary, as well as a host of other innovative and effective methods,' White Suit says, rounding off his speech.

I can't stand on my own four feet. I'm trying to stop my teeth from rattling like castanets thereby betraying my presence.

'How wonderful!' The Arch Guardian smiles and strokes his rabbit foot. 'And now, over to the head of the Information and Enlightenment sector!'

'Information for the public requires very careful handling,' announces a softly spoken middle-aged man with a double chin, a hairy mole on the tip of his nose and a shiny bald patch on the top of his head. 'We need the understanding, solidarity and support of the entire population if we want to see our efforts bear fruit. Let us not forget that a considerable proportion of our fellow citizens keep black cats as pets and it is only natural that they will try to protect them. Stray black cats are an easy target. Housecats are not. This is why we have prepared posters, leaflets and propaganda sheets with compelling slogans and catchphrases, which we intend to disperse from a hot-air balloon throughout the island. Furthermore, we have employed experienced speakers – accomplished orators – who will take it upon themselves to inform the public about the express necessity to rid our island from the bad luck brought on by black cats. We will also seek – and we hope to succeed in securing – the backing of other private organisations and even, perhaps, the support of eminent politicians.'

I'm not feeling well. My head's spinning like a top on a highly varnished parquet floor. It's not possible. They intend to wipe out the entire population of black cats. No one will be spared. By Bastet's whiskers, they've already drowned about eighty of us!

A distant roll of thunder makes me jump out of my skin. If they catch me out here I'm in danger of leaving this futile existence via the DH, PC or SC method. I panic. I run for my life. Terror-stricken, I jump from balcony to balcony, lose my balance, almost fall – no, I mustn't lose it, I must face the danger, learn as much as I can about their fiendish plans. I climb back up on to the balcony of the club, sneak a peek and find that they are all still there.

'Let's conclude our meeting with the anti-jinx hymn,' proposes the Arch Guardian.

They all stand up. They cross their fingers. The Guardian with the twirling moustache sounds a bugle. They begin to sing in unison.

Let's go forth with all our might
It is but a noble fight!
Even though the jinx has struck
We will change the nation's luck!

We'll go after each black cat
Be it scrawny or plain fat
Be it grouchy, be it sweet
From a good home or the street

Bop them one with walking sticks
With your shovels or your picks
Use a dagger or a rifle
Hold their muzzles till they stifle

For the jinx, no turning back
Rid our homes from rotten luck
Wipe them out, we all demand
And redeem our precious land!

Let's go forth with all our might
It is but a noble fight!

May our symbols give inspiration
Horseshoe and clover will save the nation!

Their voices, singing out of tune, drill into my ears; their words lash at me relentlessly. I don't want to listen any more. I don't want to think about the hamam, the steam, the rabbit foot. I can't stand watching them!

There's booming thunder again and one of the Guardians approaches the French window to see if it's raining. He sees me. Our eyes lock. He beckons to the others. About ten pairs of eyes look daggers at me. I'm doomed! They're going to skin me alive! I jump from the balcony on to a faded awning while rapid streaks of lightning tear the clouded vault of the sky, followed by the burst of a sudden downpour. I leave the Guardians of Good Luck behind me. I run away through heavy rain, drenched to the bone, my heart beating against my teeth, while all around me the rainwater pours down the eaves and gushes out of the drainpipes, the wind comes at a howling speed and flashes of lightning slash the pitch black sky.

The stain on the tie

In which a public speaker proves that black cats are to blame for the hiccups, the common cold, persistent stains and various other cat-astrophies.

The next morning, under a wild fig tree, in a garden overrun with weeds, I gave a detailed account of the incredible news to my friend Choptail. At first, he thought I'd made it all up or that I'd been hallucinating, but I finally convinced him that what I'd told him was the truth and nothing but the horrible truth!

'If what you're saying is true,' Choptail commented, 'all black cats are in grave danger; every single one of us.'

'Of course!'

'Then they all need to be informed. We should all decide together how to thwart their plans.'

'What do you suggest?'

'We'll call an emergency meeting and invite black cat delegations from every quarter, district, neighbourhood and backyard! From every alley! Every plot of land!'

'You're right. If we're united, if only we can work together, our enemies will find it much harder to harm us!' I agreed. 'If we all pool our resources, somehow we'll find a way to cope with the devious threat of the Guardians of Good Luck.'

We decided to put our plan into action as soon as possible. However, it wasn't that easy to contact all the various cats who enjoyed general esteem and, according to public opinion, possessed the qualities of a leader. Some we plainly couldn't find, some were really not convinced; others excused themselves, claiming that they had more urgent matters to attend to.

Anyway, employing the help of Purrcy, Bumpy and a few other trusted friends, we split the map between us and started spreading the word to as many cats as we could find, urging them to come to the meeting that was scheduled for the following Friday night, on the roof of an old coal shed, behind the flour mills.

In the meantime, among other things, I had taken it upon myself to inform Darren the Daring, a veteran cat with a kink in his tail and half an ear missing. He lived on a farm, a short stroll from the city.

I found him sunning himself in a barnyard, lazily draped round the rim of a dried-up well. He'd lost quite a few of his old mates from the neighbouring farms, but was blowed if he knew why. He'd been wondering – he said – what might have happened to them. When I told him in no uncertain terms what had been going on, he looked troubled and readily agreed to take part in the meeting. He promised to be there at the agreed time and date and to bring his ideas with him.

A little later, as I was making my way back to town, satisfied with the outcome of my mission, I heard a noise and shouting coming from nearby.

I approached with great caution and guess what I saw? Droves of people, crowding a ploughed field. At the front, mounted on an empty feta-cheese barrel, stood a speaker, wearing a checked jacket and an undone tie. He had flabby cheeks, red with the excitement, popped-out eyes and he raved at the top of his hoarse voice, 'My dear and sorely tried fellow citizens. Who's responsible for all the bad luck, all the suffering, all the hardships that infest this vain world?'

'Our stupidity!' quipped an urchin with dirty cheeks.

'Our sins!' shouted an old lady.

'Wrong! Come on! Something else is to blame! Come!'

'What?'

'Black cats!' shouted the speaker, with confidence.

'Are you pulling our leg, mate?' asked a sunburned farmer with a half-eaten peach in his hand. 'What have black cats got to do with the price of pickled beetroot, so to speak?'

The speaker drew a handkerchief out of his pocket and wiped his sweaty neck. 'I'm serious and I can prove it. It is all too clear and indisputable and historically documented that anything black bodes nothing but misfortune!'

'What sort of black are you talking about?' asked the farmer with the half-eaten peach.

'Black magic! Black market! Black hearts! Blacklists! Black flags! Blackheads! Blacklegs! Think of the horror of black magic! Think of the excruciating Black Death! Reflect on treacherous blacklists and the wickedness of blackmail, not to mention black markets, blackheads and blacklegs!'

The speaker stopped and with a dramatic gesture, pointed in the direction of a gentleman with a bulging stomach, wearing a tweed suit and matching waistcoat. 'You, sir, for example! You, with the stained tie. Will you be so kind as to inform us how your tie ended up in this sorry state?'

'Er . . . because I got the hiccups while I was eating beef casserole,' answered the man in question.

'Yes, yes, that may be so, but why did you get the hiccups while you were eating beef casserole and not when you were not eating beef casserole, if you please?'

'Ermm.' The man with the bulging stomach was lost for words. 'That's a tough one . . .'

'I'll tell you why!' declared the speaker, enthusiastically. 'You got the hiccups while you were eating beef casserole because, on your way to the restaurant to partake of the said beef casserole, you most certainly crossed paths with a black cat!'

'But I did not have the beef casserole at a restaurant,' came the disappointing reply, accompanied by a belch. 'My sister-in-law, Euthalia, cooked it for us at her country cottage.'

The argument about the sister-in-law did not seem to foil the speaker. 'Then, I put it to you, that while your sister-in-law was cooking it,' he said, stressing each individual word, 'a black cat must have been watching her from the kitchen window with an evil eye.'

The man with the bulging stomach loosened his tie and examined the stain with renewed interest, as if he was seeing it for the first time.

The speaker wiped the sweat from his forehead with the back of his hand and pointed at a weedy, spotty youth, who was holding a bicycle pump. 'You, young man!'

'Yes, sir?'

'Why have you got spots?'

'How should I know?' muttered the young man shyly.

'Well, I do!' The speaker silenced him. 'You've got spots because a black cat must have given you the evil eye!'

The youth scratched one of his spots with a bewildered look.

'You, Grandad, with the false teeth.' The speaker turned his attention elsewhere. 'Say, why have you lost all your own teeth? Why haven't you got even one incisor, just for show?'

The old man cupped his ear with his hand. 'What's that, sonny?'

'I said, why haven't you got any teeth, Grandad?'

'I can't hear well, laddie. Speak up a bit, God bless you.'

'Why have you lost all your teeth and why have you gone deaf, for that matter? Don't strain your brain! I'll tell you why. All this has happened because you must have come across a black cat when you were young!'

'What? *You* mind your tongue, young man. How dare you?'

'There you are, ladies and gentlemen! This is what man is reduced to when he comes across a black cat in the early years of his life!'

The crowd cast pitying looks at the old man.

The speaker drew a deep breath and went on to point at a middle-aged man in short sleeves, who was sporting a sizeable bump on his forehead.

'You, at the back . . . Yes, you with the bump. Do you know where this bump that decorates your forehead comes from?'

'I know, blast it! I owe it to a pot of hyacinths that fell off a balcony and on to my head!'

'Ah, but why did it fall, dear sir?'

'Because – because –'

'Because a cat that crossed your path put the jinx on you.'

'But – I never crossed paths with a black cat.'

'Don't *say* that! Don't! Perhaps you weren't paying enough attention. Black cats are devious. Treacherous! Cunning! It must have crossed you like a streak of lightning, before you had the chance to see or hear it!'

'Is that so, eh? Well if I had it in my hands, I'd tear it limb from limb, the dastardly beast!'

The speaker raised his voice to a howl, now. 'Fellow citizens. Who's to blame for bad luck? For all our misfortunes? For all adversities, setbacks and mishaps?'

'Black cats!' shouted some hotheads from the crowd who had got the message.

I noticed that two or three of them were wearing the familiar badge of the Guardians – the four-leafed clover.

'Who's responsible for calamities and disasters?' the speaker went on.

'Black cats!'

'Who is to blame when we slip on banana skins?'

'Black cats!'

'Who is to blame when we prick ourselves with rusty pins?'

'Black cats!'

'Who is responsible for buses running late?'

'Black cats!'

'Who is responsible when we put on weight?'

'Black cats!'

'Who is responsible when priceless crockery falls and breaks?'

'Black cats!'

'Who is to blame for tsunamis and earthquakes?'

'Black cats!'

'Who is to blame for itchy mosquito bites?'

'Black cats!'

'Who is to blame for our sleepless nights?'

'Black cats!'

'Whose fault is it if our taxes are so high?'

'Black cats!'

'Who is to blame for dark clouds in the clear sky?'

'Black cats!'

'And who is to blame for swindlers and crooks?'

'Black cats!'

'Who is behind those who cook the books?'

'Black cats!'

'Who is to blame for typhoons, landslides, flatulence and tidal waves?'

'Black cats!'

'That's right! Those wretched, cursed, good-for-nothing black cats!'

The crowd roared louder and louder. Their eyes bulged. Fists clenched. Cheeks flushed. Beads of sweat broke out on their foreheads.

'What's the solution, then?' raged the speaker, now in a state of manic elation. 'How will we put an end to these calamities?'

'Tell us! Tell us! Saviour, tell us!' begged the crowd.

'I'll tell you right now! There's only one solution! These black cats must be wiped off the face of the earth once and for all! Not a single one must be left alive!'

'Not a single one!' chanted the mob, as if in a trance. 'Not a single one!'

'What's the duty of every responsible citizen, then?' howled the speaker, raising his clenched fist.

'To exterminate black cats!' responded the frenzied crowd, the Guardians first and foremost among them.

The speaker stretched out an arm which quivered with righteous fury and pointed in the direction of the city.

'Off you go, then!' he bellowed. 'Hunt them down! Drag the cursed creatures from their hiding-places! The time has come for them to pay for the terrible sufferings they have caused, the countless misfortunes they have brought upon us!'

The crowd, eyes blazing, nostrils flaring, mouths foaming rabidly, crying hatred and revenge, spilled like a torrent towards the town.

'Forward! Go! Go!'

'Let's ferret out the evil beasts!'

'Smoke out the cursed pests!'

'The time has come to pay them back for all their heinous crimes!'

8

The cook and the cleaver

In which our hero comes face to face with a cook, who is about to shorten his life with a cleaver, when an unexpected saviour appears at the critical moment.

My own sins are few, and certainly not of the kind the infuriated mob was eager to accuse me of. The kit had to split, so I scarpered as fast as I could, before those furious fanatics found me and beat the living daylights out of me. I began a strategic retreat but in my panic, I got confused and went off in the wrong direction. I soon found myself in the last place I should have made an appearance that night – the cobbled streets of the town, which were lit by the torches of the maddened crowd. Gangs of enraged protesters were looking for black cats, chanting:

> *Wherever they hide, we will sniff them out!*
> *Wherever they turn, we will rout them out!*
> *We'll get them and teach them to mess us about!*

I saw plenty that awful night. I saw dishevelled women brandishing carving knives, children with slings, young men with spear guns, woodcutters with felling axes, butchers with meat cleavers, even drunkards clutching the necks of broken beer bottles in their hands, chasing after their four-legged prey with murder in their eyes.

I saw them break grocery shop windows that displayed tins of cat food. I saw them – their faces hideously distorted in the flickering torch light – bang on doors and menacingly ask groggy housewives if there was a black cat in their building. I saw them lie in wait on street corners with pick-axes in their hands. I saw them light fires to burn their victims alive.

I had to hide somewhere before I fell into their murderous clutches myself. I sneaked into a dark, winding alley. I could hear heavy footsteps and loud cries behind me. The alley came to a dead end at a brick wall about two metres tall. I climbed up, got my bearings, jumped and landed bang on some tins planted with carnations in a tiny paved courtyard. In front of me there was a half-open window with embroidered curtains, through which came a glimmer of light. I reached it in three silent bounds, leaped up on to the window sill and thence into a cosy kitchen. A pot was gently simmering on the stove. On the table there was a pan full of little baklava squares that smelled heavenly. I couldn't help myself – I dunked my paw into the syrup and licked it.

'Aiiii! A black cat!' I hear someone yell. I turn round and see a plump cook with rosy cheeks and blonde hair in a bun grab a soapy meat cleaver from the sink and lunge at me furiously.

I jump off the table, twist and turn, then dart between her legs and find myself in a corridor that I soon realise, to my horror, is a dead end. I turn round and see my impending doom. The cook is approaching, howling; the meat cleaver is raised above my head. She's just about to bring it down with all her might and bisect me. Boy, I'm in trouble. Only a miracle can save me now. And then it happens! Right out of the blue, a grey mouse jumps out of a mousehole, swiftly scrabbles up the cook's ankle to her knee and disappears under her voluminous petticoats. The cook lets out a piercing scream, the cleaver drops from her hand and impales itself on the wooden floor. She starts shaking her clothes out, thrashing and hobbling around as if she's dancing the Charleston on a floor strewn with sea urchins. In the corridor, two doors open simultaneously. At one of them there's a baffled octagenarian with his trousers at half-mast, holding a roll of toilet paper in his hand, and at the other door there peeps out a sleepy bald man wearing pyjamas the colour of fish roe, clutching a hot-water bottle.

The mouse drops from the cook's skirt on to the wooden floor and scuttles towards me. I recognise him immediately. It's my old mate Cheapskate.

'This way!' he beckons, and guides me through the

bedroom, dimly lit by a gas lamp, to a wide open window and from there to a vegetable garden planted with parsnips, artichokes and aubergines.

'What are you doing here?' I asked him a few moments later when, hidden under the broad leaves of an artichoke, we manage to catch our breath.

'What do you mean, what am I doing here? I live next door. The house of Peter Pentameter, the poet, is just down the block. But boy, Madame Bebelescu has got some smashing cheeses in her cellar! Simply dee-licious!'

'Who's Madame Bebelescu?'

'The one with the rosy cheeks who was after you with a meat cleaver only just now! I pay her a visit quite often to sample her cheeses. Her husband, the bald one with the hot-water bottle, is a wealthy cheese merchant, if you please, and her father-in-law has shares in seven cheese-pie shops. Lovely family! Ooh, I almost forgot! I've got you a fantastic new verse for your girl. Listen:

> *Cheese may melt, too*
> *And turn into fondue*
> *But babe, my love for you*
> *Forever will be true!*

'Good one, innit?'

'Yeah, yeah, it's good and incredibly romantic, but I've

got other fish to fry at the moment.'

'What's up, then? Spill the beans!'

'You mean you don't know?'

'Erm ... right ... Black cats are under persecution. Hallelujah! Oops! Sorry! Forgot you're a black cat.'

'Well, *I* can't forget it!'

'Stiff upper lip, mate! It will soon blow over. You could have been a mouse – they'd be after you forever! Round the clock! Well, thank God for mouseholes. And by the way, some sizzling hot piece of information has come my way, which might interest you.'

'Fire away!'

'See, this mate of mine, Rocky Roquefort, alias Scaramouse, lives in a stately mousehole in the house of Guillaume De La Bogue, who's the Arch Guardian of Good Luck.'

'You're kidding!'

'Mouse's honour!'

'Go on!'

'Well, Scaramouse happened to overhear that the host, that is Guillaume De La Bogue, is giving a formal dinner party and he has invited the Prime Minister and a number of other eminent persons, like the Minister of Public Order and a couple of businessmen who run a company under the name IMT in order to secure their support in his campaign against bad luck.'

'Are you sure?'

'Of course I'm sure.'

I thought about this for a while. My brain was in overdrive. The more we knew about their plans, I concluded, the better.

'You know what, Cheapskate? I'd really like to watch this meeting at De La Bogue's house. How about it? Can you find a way to get me in?'

'Yeah, sure, of course. I've got it all worked out. Am I a friend or what, eh?'

I nearly kissed him. 'Say then . . . what's the deal?'

'In the dining room, where dinner will be served, there's a mahogany sideboard that stands on four legs – so there's some space between the floor and its bottom. I've set things up so you can slip into the dining room without anyone seeing you, hide under the sideboard and watch the goings-on undetected.'

'Thanks, Cheapskate, mate. You're a real friend. Now, tell me all there is to know!'

'One moment. Listen to this first . . .

> *'There are sorrows in each love affair,*
> *As there are holes in Swiss gruyere.'*

I did not pay enough attention at the time, but that little ditty was to prove prophetic.

Having exhausted his poetic repertoire, Cheapskate finally gave me the details I needed to hide in Guillaume De La Bogue's house and attend the conspirators' dinner undisturbed. Then we said goodbye and went our separate ways without any further unexpected events.

9

The conspirators' dinner

*In which our hero, hidden under a sideboard, listens
to a crucial discussion amongst very important people.*

On the appointed day, based on the priceless information imparted to me by Cheapskate, I was curled
up under a heavy antique sideboard in a very posh dining
room with a priceless thick Persian carpet. From my hiding
place, I had a perfect view of the entire room and I could
listen unobserved.

The walls were covered with deep burgundy wallpaper.
On one of them was a huge Venetian mirror, while the other
three were decorated with sabres, daggers, spears, swords,
halberds and other rare weapons from the host's collection.
About ten solemn and unsmiling dinner guests sat round a
long, narrow mahogany table with carved lion's feet, which
was laid with an embroidered linen tablecloth. The china
dinner service, the elaborate candlesticks and the sterling
silver cutlery gleamed in the light of seven gilt chandeliers.

Three immaculate waiters with pointed chins and powdered wigs solemnly carried in one exquisite dish after another. The meal started with a clear consommé of bonito, followed by smoked mussels garnished with finely chopped radishes, lobster simmered in coconut milk and crayfish spiced with paprika. I must confess that my mouth was watering. I do not know how I managed to refrain from leaping into the soup tureen with the bonito consommé and letting myself drown in it in sheer bliss.

Guillaume De La Bogue, a man with wavy grey hair and a blue velvet waistcoat trimmed with delicate lace, was sitting at the head of the table. I recognised him at once. He was the Arch Guardian and I'd seen him first at the offices of the Guardians of Good Luck.

Opposite him, grim-faced and daunting, sat the Prime Minister, an elderly man with a hard, tense face and a severe air about him, dressed in black and wearing the expression of an undertaker suffering from toothache.

'So, what is your request, my dear friend?' asked the Prime Minister, as an enormous platter of golden-brown roast pheasant – flavoured with rosemary and garnished with plum jelly and mint leaves – was placed in the middle of the table.

'We wish to beg the government's cooperation in our fight against bad luck,' answered Guillaume De La Bogue, as an elegant waiter filled his glass with pink champagne.

'In other words?'

'We hope that you will help us wipe out all the black cats in the land!'

The Prime Minister plunged his fork into a morsel of pheasant. 'I am sorry to disappoint you,' he said, as he lifted it to his mouth, 'but at this time, there are far more serious matters demanding our attention.'

'Such as . . . ?' Monsieur Guillaume De La Bogue enquired politely. 'Would you be kind enough to enlighten me?'

'By all means. Unemployment, inflation, the devaluation of the currency, the national debt, the unfavourable balance of payments,' recited the Finance Minister with a frown; he was an experienced politician who looked like a sulky mummy with his thin hair and long, sallow face.

'Hospital queues. Miners' strikes. Walkouts at textile mills,' continued the Minster of Labour, a little old man with a moustache that curled at the tips, and a white beard that flowed in waves over his purple waistcoat.

'A soaring crime rate, burglaries, robberies, briberies, kidnappings and blackmail,' added the Minister of Justice, whose wavy hair shone with brilliantine, but not as brightly as the precious gold and sapphire pin decorating his tie.

'Marches, demonstrations, riots,' added the Minister of Public Order, a stout man, with auburn side whiskers, who then burped discretely.

'As you can see, with problems of such gravity, however much we would like to, we have no time to occupy ourselves with cats,' said the Prime Minister with an air of finality.

'If you understood your own best interests, yes, you would indeed occupy yourselves with cats.' The host's voice sounded blunt and decisive.

'What do you mean, Monsieur De La Bogue? What possible connections can there be between cats and the intractable problems faced by the government?' enquired the Prime Minister, a hint of irritation in his voice.

'There's a direct connection! Yes! Have no doubt your Excellency! Black cats can be of great use to you! I do not exaggerate if I say that they may be your salvation – literally! They can even guarantee your re-election!'

'You are joking, of course, Monsieur De La Bogue,' said the Finance Minister, laughing and using an ivory toothpick to extract a bead of black caviar that had got wedged between two of his gold teeth.

'Not in the least. I never joke about matters of such gravity,' answered Guillaume De La Bogue calmly. 'Let me put my cards on the table, gentlemen. As you yourselves admit, the government is facing serious, perhaps insurmountable, problems. And as if this were not enough, elections are just round the corner. Correct me if I am wrong, but all the polls indicate that your chances of winning the election are slim – demonstrations, protests, rallies and strikes are rife, as you yourselves just admitted. You will most probably lose.'

'Unfortunately, we cannot discount that unpleasant possibility,' confessed the Minister of Finance, and stopped munching a crisp croquette, his appetite suddenly gone. At that moment, however, a waiter set down on the table a dish of roast venison in a spicy blackberry sauce, and the minister's appetite returned immediately.

'But what if voters did not consider the ills of the country to be the fault of your incompetent administration?' continued the host. 'If they did not blame the government for the failure of its economic and social policies? If voters believed that you were not to blame for whatever was wrong with the nation, but that someone else was responsible?'

'Who?' asked the Minister of Public Order.

'Black cats!'

The Prime Minister, who at that moment was swallowing a blackberry, nearly choked. He went bright red and started to cough. Fortunately, the Finance Minister thumped him hard on the back three or four times and the blackberry flew out of his mouth and sank into a glass filled to the brim with frothy champagne. A waiter discreetly removed the glass and replaced it with a new one.

The Prime Minister drew breath, took a sip of champagne and recovered. 'What would happen if people believed black cats were to blame?' he asked, dabbing the spicy blackberry sauce off his lips and chin with a linen napkin.

'Instead of blaming you, they would take their anger out on black cats.'

'Correct! That is where people's rage must be channelled,' agreed twin businessmen with small, cunning eyes sunk in folds of fat and bulging pear-shaped bellies, who, I knew from the introductions that had taken place earlier, were called Ernest and Edmund De La Dupe. They ran a business by the name of IMT. 'If you do not want to lose votes, you have great need of black cats.'

'I am not sure I fully understand you. Could you please elaborate, gentlemen?' The voice of the Prime Minister barely concealed his interest.

'It's very simple! Extremely simple,' explained Guillaume De La Bogue, putting six quail eggs on his plate and an equal number of sea-turtle tongues. 'Who, for example, can say with any certainty, that on the day the most honourable Finance Minister was forced to devalue the currency, a black cat had not crossed his path? Who can rule out the possibility that, on the day our industrious Minister of Foreign Affairs was about to enter into a tricky negotiation with neighbouring states, he hadn't run into a dozen black cats? Who could deny that, I ask you?'

'In other words, you mean to say that if there were no black cats, everything would have gone like clockwork?' asked the Prime Minister with increasing interest.

'This is precisely what I mean!' De La Bogue assured him.

There was silence for a few minutes. The dinner guests ate quietly, sunk in thought. Even the waiters walked around on tiptoe so as not to disturb the diners' cogitations.

'Now that I think of it, you may well be right.' The Prime Minister broke the silence, in a voice shaking slightly with emotion. 'The government began to go downhill that very morning when an insolent black cat threw itself in front of my limousine, and I nearly ran over its tail, if I'm not mistaken.'

'You see, dear Prime Minister, I knew you would remember!' Monsieur De La Bogue smiled brightly, glowing with satisfaction. 'I was more than certain that something like that had happened!'

'I wish I had!'

'You wish you had what?'

'Run over its tail! I wish I had rooted the evil out then!' the Prime Minister burst out. He beckoned a waiter to fill up his glass, and continued, 'You will have my government's unreserved cooperation in your righteous struggle to improve living conditions in this country.'

'All newspapers friendly to the government and all the state information services will be placed at your disposal,' declared the Minister of Public Order, and moaned with pleasure, his eyes closed, as he swallowed a mouthful of roast venison.

'Our company, IMT, will make a generous contribution

to your party to help finance this crucial and beneficial campaign,' announced the twin businessmen in unison.

'People will hear the words "black cat" and they will go berserk!' the Minister of Labour assured his fellow diners festively. 'Black cats will be held responsible for low pensions. Black cats will be blamed for run-down schools. Black cats will be accused of tampering with food! Black cats will take the rap for bribe-giving, bribe-taking and all corruption!'

'And we'll be triumphantly re-elected because we will promise to rid our country of black cats once and for all! Every single one of them!' rounded off the Prime Minister.

'Exactly! But let us not forget however, gentlemen, that this is not only our own but also every responsible and conscientious citizen's duty!' thundered the excited Minister for Justice.

'You know, some of our fellow countrymen do love their black cats. It will be difficult for them to denounce or exterminate them,' came De La Bogue's insidious remark.

'No matter how difficult it may prove, how painful and unpleasant, they will have to do it! It is their patriotic duty!' declared the Minister of Public Order and hit the table with his fist, sending three peas dripping with thick sauce bouncing off his plate. The first pea got stuck on a piece of crystal on the chandelier, the second landed on the shiny, brilliantined curls of the Minister of Justice, and the third one balanced on the tip of the nose of the Finance Minister for a moment before it rolled on to the tablecloth and then off the table. A waiter with a pointed nose bent over and started looking for it as discreetly as he could.

'If they do not fulfill their duty, if they do not denounce their black cats, they will have their property confiscated!' decided the Finance Minister, and his face lit up at the prospect of additional income and the copious flow of cash heading for the Treasury.

'I was quite sure that, in the end, being the astute politicians that you are, you would all see things from the right perspective!' Their host smiled, visibly gratified.

And with these words he beckoned the waiters to place on the table three platters with caramellised spiced bananas, strawberries flambé and a gently quivering quince jelly gateaux.

'And now, gentlemen,' he concluded, 'let us enjoy our dessert.'

10

Trapped in the greenhouse

*In which a pea is the cause for countless cat-astrophes
and our hero experiences hallucinations in a tropical
greenhouse.*

In the meantime, the waiter with the pointed nose was bent
on discovering the rogue pea, which, as if on purpose, had
rolled under the sideboard and was resting right beside me. If
the waiter decided to look under the sideboard, he would
definitely get wind of my presence there and not even an
earthquake could save me then.

So I give the pea a little push with my paw to make it roll
towards him. He sees it and is about to grab it but it slips
through his fingers and rolls back to me as if I were a feline
pea-magnet. I can see his white-gloved hand fumble for it
close to me. I draw myself as far away as possible, which is
not far enough, as it seems, because one finger tickles my
whiskers. I try, I try hard, but I can't help myself any more
and out bursts an almighty sneeze.

68

·68·

'*Aaaaaaachooooo!*'

I pray quietly that he might not have heard it, but he has. I feel the white-gloved hand seize me by the tail and pull at it forcefully. Now, nothing hurts a cat so much as having someone drag it by the tail. Wild with pain, I try to dig my teeth or claws into something for resistance. I scratch the Persian carpet and, in a mad dash, I hook my nails on the linen tablecloth, which hangs almost down to the floor, and drag it behind me, complete with plates, serving platters, cutlery, glassware, soup tureens, bottles of champagne and fruit bowls. The diners spring up from their seats to avoid the torrent of crockery. As the Minister of Labour jumps up, his chair pushes the waiter, who lets go of my tail for a moment, which gives me the chance to get away, leap on to his head and from there, perform a high jump and hang myself from the dangling cut-glass crystals of the chandelier, which starts to sway, like a pendulum.

The Minister of Public Order, who's not far from having a stroke, climbs on to the table to try and pull me down from the chandelier and restore order but it all ends in disaster because the legs of his trousers go up in flames, being too close for comfort to the flambé of strawberries.

The Prime Minister, displaying exemplary presence of mind, hastens to give him a hand by emptying the contents of the champagne cooler over his person, but misses by a whisker and hits the two enraged IMT businessmen, who have each taken hold of a cream cake and are about to hurl them at me, but, blinded by the ice-cold water, they miss their mark and the cream cakes land bang on the face of Guillaume De La Bogue, who now looks as if he's got a head of whipped cream and two glacé cherries for eyes. Meanwhile, the head waiter has brought in a rope ladder and is struggling to reach up to the chandelier, while another waiter is doing his best to unplug a banana that has got stuck up the right nostril of the Minister of Justice. The third waiter threatens to dismember me with a double-bladed axe from De La Bogue's collection of rare weapons. Instead of finding its target, the axe cuts one of the cords of the chandelier in half and the waiter is electrified. The same fate awaits the other two who rush to his aid, which results in all three waiters giving off bluish sparks and flashes in perfect synchronicity.

As for me, not really knowing what I'm doing, I jump off the chandelier on to the table as it topples over and come face to face with a delirious Guillaume De La Bogue who's after my blood, brandishing a gleaming scimitar from his collection. Luckily for me, he steps on to a piece of quince jelly, slips forward and instead of slashing my throat, the scimitar cuts the braces of the terrified Prime Minister, whose trousers drop into a small pool of blackberry sauce and pink champagne that has been soaking into the Persian carpet – which is already up in flames, by the way, from the flambé of strawberries. The Venetian mirror shatters into a thousand pieces, hit by a stray champagne bottle, kicked by one of the waiters who are still throwing out sparks like a firework display.

'What did I tell you? They're jinxes! Didn't I tell you?' are the last words I hear in the ongoing pandemonium, before I shoot out of the dining room and make myself scarce, following, in reverse, the route Cheapskate's friend had advised. I go down to the cellar and from there, via the coal shute, dart out into the garden.

As I run past the blooming flowerbeds, I see a gardener approaching, holding a pot of blue hydrangeas in his arms.

That's all I need now! I think to myself.

I turn right and hide in a glass greenhouse heavy with the scent of tropical flowers. Fortunately, the gardener is none the wiser as he comes into the greenhouse, puts some hydrangeas down next to some gladioli, and goes out again, closing the door behind him. *Now* I'm in the soup! There's no way out.

The day goes, it gets dark, it's light and then it's dark again, and I'm still there, trapped in the greenhouse. I'm terribly thirsty so I drink from a small basin and, to appease my hunger, I am forced to chew on the fleshy petals of some tropical flowers. Most of them have a vile, bitter taste. Some are juicy and tasty but they make me drowsy and – worse, still – delusional. I see Cuddles the bulldog serenade me with a mandolin, I see the Prime Minister drive his limousine at me, sounding his horn, bent on crushing my tail, I see the three waiters as jugglers in a circus, tossing bowls of strawberry flambé in the air, I see my best mate, Choptail, serenade Abigail, the cat with the most lovely tail. I'm sinking. I'm wasted. I'm a bird flying high in the air, swooping down towards the earth. I'm a black seagull!

Every time the gardener opens the door, I'm in such deep torpor that I can hardly drag my paws. The days go by. From time to time, I remember about the meeting at the coal shed. I reckon it must be tomorrow. If I don't manage to get out of the greenhouse, I'll miss it for sure. I decide to fast so as to be in my right mind when the gardener opens the door next time. It is kind of hard, though, because I have grown used to eating those petals, but I battle with hunger and withdrawal symptoms, and when the gardener opens the door, I run for it.

I thought I might be able to slip out undetected, but he catches sight of me! He is taken aback! A pot of hydrangeas slips out of his hands and crashes on to my tail, which has still not recovered from the waiter's kind attentions. The pain's killing me but I waste no time nursing the wound. I make a screaming dash for it, dart out of the greenhouse and run like the wind.

11

Graziella's engagement

In which our hero seeks comfort in the arms of his beloved, but his feelings are far from reciprocated.

O nce I'd put sufficient distance between myself and Guillaume De La Bogue's villa, I collapsed in a ditch filled with dry autumn leaves and licked my throbbing tail, until I drifted into a deep, untroubled sleep.

When I woke up, I felt an urgent need for a little loving tenderness. Why deny it? I'd missed Graziella terribly. What with all the infernal things that had happened, one right on top of the other, I had neglected my sweetheart and had even failed to show any signs of life. My purrcious would be worried sick and was entitled to give me a good ticking off or even sulk a little.

The last thing I wanted was to upset her but it seemed I couldn't do otherwise. I had to tell her about the persecution and the incredible danger I was in, as well as of my heroic, superfeline efforts to survive. I could just picture her excited face as she listened to a detailed account of my exploits, only too eager to ease my pain with her tender touch. I looked at the sky. It was still early morning, I had plenty of time to visit my purrcious and then go to the coal shed to find out what all we black cats could achieve united. So I made my way to the mansion with the oleanders and the pomegranate trees once more.

It was a glorious day. Children played merrily in the schoolyards. Milkmen merrily placed glass bottles of milk on doorsteps. Housewives put the washing out on the line to dry in the light breeze. There was no portent of the tragic turn that things would take that very night. But still, the signs were already there, all around me. I couldn't help but notice that the traffic police had put up brand new signposts at street crossings that read:

PEDESTRIANS BEWARE
OF BLACK CATS!

I also noticed that all the newspapers displayed at the news-stands had similar titles:

INTERIOR MINISTER'S SHOCK PLEA:
CRUSH ISLAND'S CAT SCOURGE!

NO HOPE FOR ECONOMIC RECOVERY TILL

BLACK CATS ROUTED
FROM ISLAND FOR GOOD

MINISTER OF PUBLIC AFFAIRS WARNS:
CONFISCATION OF PROPERTY FOR
CAT SYMPATHISERS

If that was not enough, there were several men with long
brushes and buckets of glue, whistling nonchalantly as they
put up signs with equally comforting messages. A red poster
with black letters said:

WANTED!!!
BLACK CATS

Further down the wall there was another poster, even worse
than the previous one.

NOTICE TO ALL LAW-ABIDING CITIZENS:
ONE LUCKY HORSESHOE
FOR EVERY CAT TAIL
HANDED OVER TO THE AUTHORITIES

Every inch of a fence opposite a school was plastered with
posters with huge, screaming letters:

IT IS EVERY PUPIL'S OBLIGATION
TO RAT ON A BLACK CAT
AND SAVE THE NATION

That was too much! I jumped on to the fence, looked around carefully to make sure that no one was watching and peed all over the poster.

The remainder of my journey was uneventful. I arrived at the manor where my beloved lived and slipped quietly into the blossoming garden. The flowers smelled heavenly, a few golden sun rays played on the mirror-like surface of the pond with the goldfish and the morning dew sparkled on the deep green of the lawn. Cuddles, as usual, was fast asleep outside his little wooden house, his ugly mug resting on his front paws. I climbed cheerfully on to a pomegranate tree, whose leaves rustled in the morning breeze, and let out my signal meow. Dead quiet. I meowed again. Nothing. Graziella failed to make an appearance. I tried the love-call three more times and then I meowed twice in irritation, but to no avail. My darling failed to respond. I could smell something fishy.

She wouldn't have gone completely deaf, now, would she? I asked myself.

As you may already know, Angora cats are a little bit deaf and it wouldn't take much for one to go altogether stone deaf. I let out one or two long, desperate, heart-rending mews, at the danger of waking up Cuddles, until, lo and behold, my chosen one appeared from among the oleanders and swayed towards me more beautiful than ever.

'What's got into you? Why are you mewing like that?' she asked in a way that was far from endearing.

She'd never criticised my mewing before, which, to tell the honest truth, may have lacked in melody but scored very high points for vigour.

'How am I mewing then?' I protested.

'Loudly, irritatingly and with total disregard for public peace and quiet! Can't you see you're embarrassing me?'

It was obviously not one of her good days. 'What do you mean I'm embarrassing you?' I asked, bitterly disappointed with this terse reception.

She climbed up the pomegranate tree without rubbing herself against me, as she used to do in the past, without licking me with her rosy tongue, without making a fuss over me.

'You know very well what I mean! Come on, out with it! What are you doing here? What is the purpose of your visit? I'm listening!'

I was hurt. It was the first time she had ever snapped at me like this. I felt as if someone had emptied a bucket of ice over my head. Nevertheless, I did not let my disappointment show.

'I thought, purrcious,' I began coyly, 'that maybe the news about the persecution of black cats had reached you and so I came to reassure you that, as you can see, I am safe and sound and that there is not the slightest need for you to worry.'

'Worry?' she ticked me off. 'How can I not worry? How is it possible not to worry about you?'

I liked that. She was worried about me. That was a good sign. You only worry about those you love. For those you don't, you don't give a toss.

'No, no, no, no, no!' I soothed her 'Relax! I assure you that I'll manage all right. I'm one smart cat, me. I know how to protect myself, how to twist and turn and avoid pitfalls! Don't you worry about me!'

'I'm not worried about you!' she interrupted, haughtily.

'Who are you worried about, then?' I wondered aloud. 'Cuddles? Do you think he might look at himself in the mirror and have a heart attack.'

'Oh, don't be facetious, please! I'm anxious about my future.'

'What about your future?'

'Don't you realise that your antics are putting me in danger?'

'What kind of danger?'

'Don't pretend you don't know. Haven't you heard? Anyone who associates with a black cat is considered a suspect for dealing with the dark forces and is arrested by special armed patrols. Don't you care about me at all? What will happen if anyone sees us together? Can you answer that?'

'But –' I tried to explain. She wouldn't let me speak.

'You may even drag my owners down,' she went on

fiercely. 'What have the poor people done to you? They may get into trouble for no reason at all! Those thugs may even torch the villa! They've already burned down two houses and a knitting yarn warehouse, and that's in our neighbourhood alone!'

I couldn't believe my ears! I scratched one ear first and then the other in case it did them some good.

'What do you mean?' I asked.

'We must . . .' She hesitated.

'We must what?'

'We must stop seeing each other.'

I hadn't seen that coming. 'For how long?'

'I don't know. For some time. Until things calm down.'

'I don't see that things will calm down. In fact, they're likely to get worse.'

'Then it's best if you go before the situation becomes irreverent.'

'You mean irreversible.'

'Whatever.'

'And what about our love? Our dreams? The vows we pledged to each other under the moonlight? Don't you love me any more? Don't you yearn for me like I do you? Aren't you my soulmate, my puttycat, my purrcious?'

'I can't say I don't love you . . . The problem is your colour.'

'What's wrong with my colour? Come on, tell me! What's wrong with it?'

'Well, it makes me feel uncomfortable . . . uneasy . . . anxious . . . depressed.'

'You don't say? May I remind you that once upon a time you used to like it? You used to admire its lustrous sheen and say that it excited you, it fascinated, it captivated you. You used to say it drove you crazy!'

'Well, that was in the past. Things are different now. Time passes, things change and the crowds cry for revenge.'

'Graziella, dear, listen to me. Please do. Why do you pay attention to all this nonsense – all the unfounded slander you've been hearing? All that's been happening lately is so inconceivable, so absurd, so unjust that I'm sure it won't last much longer!'

'How do you know that?'

'I'll tell you a secret! Tonight, at midnight, something will happen that will change the course of things completely – I guarantee it!'

'What?'

'I've arranged to meet all the other black cats that are to be reckoned with at the coal shed behind the flour mills! We'll get organised, Graziella darling, we'll fight back, we'll come up with a plan! A great plan!'

A grasshopper jumped on to the branch of the pomegranate tree.

'I must go now,' Graziella said quietly. 'I must go and wash myself. I've got to look beautiful today. Very beautiful.'

'Why?'

'Rasmin will be here any minute now. He shouldn't find me looking less than my best.'

'What's Rasmin doing here?'

'We're getting engaged today.'

I almost lost my balance and tumbled into the goldfish pond. 'What about me?'

'My advice to you is to give yourself up. They're bound to catch you sooner or later. You won't get away. Why mess about?'

'But, purrcious! You can't be telling me all this! Surely you're joking! Tell me you're joking, purrcious!'

'I'm not your purrcious any more . . .'

'Then what are you?'

'I'm a betrothed cat who must be wary of her reputation. That's all I have to say and now, goodbye.'

She jumped off the pomegranate tree, stuck her tail up in the air and walked away with an air of wounded dignity. I watched her disappear, sublime and aloof, behind the bed of daisies that she once used to pluck to find out if I loved her. It didn't cross my mind that this would be the last time I'd ever see her.

'Graziella!' I meowed in despair. 'My darling Graziella. Come back! Don't leave me! Where are you going? Graziella! Graziellaaaaaaaaaaaaa!'

Graziella did not hear me or, rather, she pretended not to. Cuddles did, though, as my heart-rending mewing had dragged him out of his lazy slumber. He sprang up, let out a hollow growl and charged at me, groaning like a bulldozer going up a steep slope. I climbed higher up the pomegranate tree and was just about to hurl a pomegranate at him when I caught sight of a gleaming limousine pulling up right in front of the entrance to the villa. An elderly chauffeur, wearing a cap and golden stripes on his dark red coat, opened the door for Mrs Camilla Caprizioni, who looked extremely elegant in a pink outfit with a fair amount of ribbon and lace, and a stiff-backed butler, bearing a velvet cushion with the handsome Rasmin curled up on top of it.

The procession entered the flowering garden and followed the gravelled path between the immaculate flowerbeds that led to the marble steps of the villa. Mrs Caprizioni was keeping herself cool with a fan made of ostrich feathers. The butler walked slowly and gravely, a lofty expression on his face, as if he were carrying a precious crown in an imperial procession. It was the chauffeur who heard Cuddles bark as if a Spanish dancer was doing the flamenco on his tail, and rushed to see what was going on. When he saw me crouching on the pomegranate tree with my fur standing on end, he went ballistic.

'Good heavens! A black cat!' he yelled. 'She's on the pomegranate tree in the garden!'

'It's "he", actually!' I corrected him.

Before I knew what was happening, two flustered

chambermaids brandishing toilet brushes, three gardeners with their pruning knives and a cook with his ladle, still dripping hot tomato and basil soup, dashed out of the house and came after my blood as I tumbled out of the tree.

12

The lady in the canary-yellow hat

In which our hero attempts to balance on a lady's hat and a little later finds himself trapped between two groups of enraged protestors.

Shouts, barking, curses, screams! What am I to do? I slip quietly into a clay watering-can. Fortunately, they fail to see me and continue their search at the thick firethorn bushes a bit further down from where I am.

I grab the opportunity, jump out of the watering-can and into a wicker basket, then up a pomegranate tree and, from there, on to the stone wall surrounding the garden. Jumping from wall to wall, I zoom past five or six gardens and orchards, leap off the last wall and land – where do you think? – on the broad-brimmed, canary-yellow hat of the lady that happens to be driving an open-top car on the other side of the wall, at full speed.

I don't know if you have ever tried to balance yourself on

the hat of an hysterical lady who's screaming the town down and who, at the same time, is trying to drive her car with one hand, while using the other to thrash you with a strawberry-coloured purse that has opened and is spilling out lipsticks, packets of chewing gum, blushers, compact mirrors and dainty monogrammed handkerchiefs, but, I assure you, it is not easy at all.

The vehicles coming from the opposite direction brake with a screech, run into lampposts, mount the pavement and crash into kiosks. The kiosk owners jump out of their properties in terror and bump into traffic policemen who are running, tearing out their hair with rage. I jump from the canary-yellow hat on to the windscreen and from there on to the pavement and land right at the feet of a Buddhist monk who's carrying a huge Chinese vase, which slips from his arms and shatters into a thousand pieces.

It goes without saying that I run away like the wind. I'd never run with such frenzy in all my life.

So, as I'm running in a spin, what do I see? A crowd of demonstrators approaching from the nearest end of the street. The enraged protestors are holding white placards with blood-red letters that read:

TO GET A BLACK CAT
USE A BASEBALL BAT!

DESPITE THEIR HIGH PROTECTION
BLACK CATS WILL NOT ESCAPE DETECTION

Besides those cheerful placards, they're also carrying walking sticks, scythes and stakes, and are chanting:

> *'Don't be a wuss,*
> *Kill a black puss!'*

Good God! With my heart beating hard I make an about-turn and start running like mad, only, to my horror, to come face to face with another crowd of demonstrators, bigger than the first, marching in from the far end of the street. The protestors are carrying rakes, pick axes, spades and yellow placards with red-hot letters that read:

WORKERS AND FARMERS UNITE!
AGAINST BLACK CATS WE FIGHT!
DON'T HOLD BACK YOUR SPITE –
LET'S DO THEM IN TONIGHT!

FRIEND, DON'T TURN YOUR BACK –
BLACK CATS BRING BAD LUCK!

They're also marching towards me, shouting:

> *'Stop the jinx today*
> *Bump off a black stray!'*

I can't believe this is happening! I'm trapped between two groups of enraged demonstrators. The one is bent on bumping off black cats, the other on using their baseball bats in a very imaginative way. And poor, wretched me, standing there, in the middle of the street, as black as coal tar, more conspicuous than a shooting target at a fairground. I'm frozen with fear. I daren't move either way. Besides, where can I go? The situation is as bad in front as it is behind me. I am actually caught between a rock and a hard place or, rather, between a scythe and a pickaxe. Their voices become louder . . .

> *'Don't be a wuss,*
> *Kill a black puss!'*

> *'Stop the jinx today*
> *Bump off a black stray!'*

And then, the inevitable happens. A club-bearing demonstrator becomes aware of my presence! I'm trying hard to pretend I'm just a black stain on the asphalt, but it doesn't work. He points at me. The voices are hushed for a split second. It's dead silent. Thousands of murderous eyes are trained on me.

'I'm not a real black cat! I'm an optical illusion!' I meow. They don't believe me for a moment.

'Please have mercy on me!' I meow again, in sheer panic.

They don't feel sorry for me! There's no pity in their glaring eyes. Screaming, cursing and yelling, they charge at me from both sides. Panic-stricken, I turn round once, arch my back, hissing and spitting with all my force to frighten them, but they're not intimidated! They keep coming closer and closer, brandishing spades and scythes, wielding sticks and stakes, waving mattocks, cleavers, clubs and axes! In my despair I look all around me, in case I can find a way out, an exit to salvation, and then, right there, on the pavement, I glimpse a half-open manhole cover that leads to the sewer. I jump desperately into the dark hole, tumble down a slippery pipe and find myself lying dizzily in a damp, mouldy tunnel. A little further down, there are three rats, shooting craps. They look at me sideways as I dart past them but say nothing. I keep on running . . .

13

Tarmac and the black stone

*In which a desperate black cat is about to jump to his
death and the Society for the Protection of Animals
changes both its name and its function.*

I roamed the maze of the city sewers for hours. I lost my
way a thousand times in murky tunnels and derelict
catacombs. I ran into giant rats with long tails who eyed me
with suspicion. Some rats were training with dumb-bells,
some were dividing stolen toys among themselves and others
were grilling hot chilli peppers on sewer gridirons.
Fortunately, they did not feel like having a go at me. What's
more, two rats winked at me slyly from behind a pile of
moulding lemon rinds and beckoned me to go near them. I
ignored them and went on my way.

I was beginning to lose track of time when at last I made
out a dim light at the end of a dark tunnel. I went closer and
soon found out that the light was coming from a grating with
some of its bars missing. I clambered up a slippery iron

ladder that was beginning to rust with all the dirty water dripping over it, surfaced and found myself in a solitary lane near a small chapel.

I had barely emerged from the sewer when I heard the voice of a newspaper-seller crying out, 'Special edition! Whoever offers a black cat sanctuary will be charged with high treason! Special editiooooooon . . .'

I couldn't believe my ears! Things were going from bad to worse. I decided there and then that it would be wiser to avoid all main streets, so as to minimise my chances of running into yet another cat-hater demonstration.

I vaulted over a whitewashed wall, took a shortcut through a garden with pansies and further down, on top of a building site, a comrade caught my eye. He was black, too. Pitch black. He had tied what looked like a black stone round his neck and was balancing on the edge of a shaky plank, ready to plunge to his death. Later, I found out that many cats could not stand the persecution and had reached the point of committing such desperate acts. One cat, by the name of Hunnikins, for example, had eaten seven spoilt sardines in a deliberate attempt to poison herself, and another, whose name was Calypso, had dunked her head into a goldfish bowl to drown. Fortunately, a goldfish obligingly bit her nose and she was saved.

I couldn't let one of our own waste his life just like that. I climbed up the scaffolding hastily and reached the cat with the stone round his neck. It was quite windy up there, the planks creaked and the wind howled in my ears.

'What are you doing there, mate?' I yelled.

'I'm knitting a sweater,' came the sarcastic reply. 'Don't you see? I'm just about to put an end to my life!'

'What for?'

'I'm riddled with guilt.'

'Why? What have you done? Did you scratch the archbishop by any chance?'

'No, I did not scratch any archbishop nor a deacon for that matter. But, as you see my friend, I happen to be black.'

'So what? Why is it so bad that you're black?'

'You're asking me? Black cats are responsible for all the suffering on this poor island.'

'Whoa, hold your fleas, mate! Don't tell me that you, too, believe all this malarkey those loonies are propagating?'

'Why shouldn't I believe them? Wherever I go that's all I hear! It's on the posters! It's in the newspapers! It's broadcast on the radio! Grown-ups shout it! Children parrot it! The whole town cries it! From morning till night and from night till dawn!'

'So what? Wake up! It doesn't mean it's true just because everyone is saying it. That's not the real truth! The truth is different!'

'What good is a truth that everyone denies? What's it worth? Can you tell me? No! No! I'm an unwanted, unworthy, useless cat. At times I think I even jinx myself. Enough is enough!'

And with these words he poised himself to jump. I caught him by the tail just in time and restrained him. 'Half a minute, bro. Just half a minute!'

'Let me jump, please! Don't keep interrupting!'

'What's your name?' I played for time.

'Tarmac. Not much of a name, is it? As if everything else wasn't enough, I've got an ugly name!'

'It's as fine a name as any! Now, try to think clearly, Tarmac! Not smudged with tar, but clearly! As clearly as you can! What harm have you done?'

'Just the fact that I exist is quite enough. If so many people say so, they surely must know something.'

'Here we go again. A lie is a lie, no matter how many people believe it. Put that into your head. It isn't so difficult to grasp.'

'A lie that everyone believes is no different from a truth. It's got exactly the same consequences and the pain it causes you is real enough! In other words, a forged truth is no different at all from a real lie.'

'Look, Tarmac. I'm not sure you're thinking that clearly. You need some fresh air to clear your mind. What do you say to a walk in the countryside? It won't take us –'

He didn't let me finish my sentence. 'Truth doesn't count for much these days. Anyway, whichever way you see it, I'm not too keen on living.'

'Why?'

'Need you ask? I can't – I can't stand waiting for the moment when a hoodlum will bash my head in or, even worse, a friend will betray me. It's as if they're killing me every day, again and again, a thousand times! I'd rather decide how I go myself! Once and for all. The moment *I* choose! Goodbye, then. Thank you for your interest and for your good intention. I'll remember you for as long as I live. Goodbyeeeeee . . .'

With these words, and before I could stop him, Tarmac jumped. I shut my eyes tight. I could hear the wind whistling in my ears. I heard a distant thud. That was it . . . When I opened my eyes, though, I saw Tarmac climbing back up the scaffolding in one piece, with the stone still tied round his neck.

'I'm useless! I'm unlucky! I'm impossible! I'm to be pitied,' he whined when he arrived by my side. 'The stone I tied around my neck wasn't suitable, it appears, for my purposes.'

'Why? What kind of stone was it?'

'Pumice. It was covered in tar, though, and I couldn't tell . . .'

I tried to contain my laughter.

'And I kept asking myself, "Why does it feel so light? Why does it feel so comfortable?" Will you please help me find a more suitable stone? A weighty one?'

By now, I couldn't control myself any longer. He started to laugh, as well. The more the one laughed, the more the other laughed, too. We rolled about the scaffolding in danger of falling off, laughing ourselves silly.

'Hey, look at that!' he pointed.

Down below us we saw a bill-sticker whistling softly as he was putting up posters with the usual slogans on the wall of a school:

HEROIC CHILDREN –
YOUR COUNTRY NEEDS
YOU!

REWARD
FOR EVERY BLACK CAT
DELIVERED TO THE AUTHORITIES
THIRTY LOLLIPOPS
IN THE FOLLOWING FLAVOURS:
STRAWBERRY, MINT AND BLACKCURRANT

Tarmac winked in the direction of a bucket filled with black paint, balanced precariously on the edge of a nearby plank. There was no need for explanations, I knew immediately what he had in mind. With perfect synchronicity we made a dash for the bucket and gave it a mighty push. It moved, it swayed, fell off and landed squarely on to the head of the bill-sticker, showering him from top to toe with black paint. We shrieked with laughter as we watched him jerk about, trying to get his head out of the bucket.

'I just thought of something,' Tarmac said suddenly.

'What?'

'I know who can help us.'

'Who?'

'Have you ever heard of the Society for the Protection of Animals?'

'Now that you say it, yes, I think I've heard about them.'

'What do you think? Wouldn't they be interested to learn what we are going through?'

'You're right! It isn't a bad idea. Let's go and see!'

'Right now?'

'Why waste time? Let's go find them and tell them that we are animals and we are in urgent need of protection.'

'Yeah ... yeah ... Let's tell them we also need lots of cream, a warm fireplace, a few cuddles and the rest.'

Asking here and there, we arrived at the offices of the SPA, an isolated, neglected building, surrounded by an orchard with almond trees. The plaster decorations of the façade were crumbling. Wide steps led to the front entrance, which was flanked by two big potted palm trees.

At last! I thought. Our troubles are over! We'll find justice, here!

We climbed the steps but when we reached the top, we stopped dead in our tracks. Someone had crossed over the sign that said:

THE SOCIETY
FOR THE PROTECTION OF ANIMALS

And had written below:

THE SOCIETY
FOR THE PROTECTION OF HUMANS
FROM BLACK CATS

We were staring at the sign in horror, when the door opened and a tall, lanky young man with small glasses and a blond moustache, who was seeing off two visitors with protruding pear-shaped bellies, appeared at the opening. I recognised them at once. They were Ernest and Edmund De La Dupe, the twin directors of IMT whom I'd first seen at Guillaume De La Bogue's mansion on the day of the disastrous dinner party. IMT – I wondered what the strange initials meant.

I signalled to Tarmac. We managed to hide behind the potted palm trees just in time.

'We can't thank you enough for your new donation,' said the lanky young man with the glasses, bowing deeply to the two men. 'Your generosity is touching. We'll revamp the building and proclaim you grand benefactors. A thousand thanks, gentlemen. A thousand thanks!'

'There is absolutely no reason for you to thank us,' protested Ernest De La Dupe.

'We're glad we are in a position to make a contribution to the community!' added Edmund De La Dupe.

They'd reached the steps when their host stopped them. 'A moment, please . . . How would you prefer your name to appear on the commemorative plaque? Etched on green marble or embossed in gilt letters on top-quality brass?'

The De La Dupe twins hesitated for a couple of minutes, trying, so it seemed, to visualise both versions of the commemorative plaques. The lanky man understood their indecisiveness and volunteered to help.

'What about two plaques? A marble one on the left of the door and a brass one on the right?'

'An excellent idea, young man,' beamed Edmund De La Dupe.

'You've got a bright future ahead of you,' added Ernest De La Dupe. 'If you ever find yourself in need of a job, don't hesitate to put in an application with our firm.'

The young man thanked them and bade them farewell with such a deep bow that his nose collided with the top step forcefully, squashing an unfortunate ant, who had happened to be passing by. Who knows how many little ants had just been made orphans?

When the front door of the former SPA closed and we found ourselves alone, I saw that the familiar look of sorrow had returned in the eyes of Tarmac.

'Well, I never!' he said with a bitter smile. 'The SPA has changed its name just like that.'

'And its purpose,' I added. 'Sign of the times . . .'

We remained silent for a while. From the house next door we could hear someone playing a sonata on a piano. I tried to keep my spirits up.

'Don't worry, Tarmac, mate!' I comforted him. 'We won't let this injustice pass.'

'What are we going to do, then?'

I told him about the black cats' night meeting on the roof of the coal shed and promised to keep him informed of the results. 'United we'll confront every threat!' I assured him.

And when the news reaches Graziella, she'll forget all about Rasmin, in a flash! I thought to myself. She'll feel bitterly sorry about all this and will humbly apologise for the way she treated me and it'll be at least twelve minutes before I grant her forgiveness . . .

My optimism was contagious.

'You're right,' said Tarmac with uplifted spirits before he said goodbye. 'It's a good thing you made me change my mind! I won't do them the favour of disappearing from the face of the earth like that. No, sir! If they don't like me, let them take me on. But there's one thing I guarantee. If they are after my hide, my fabulous black hide, they'll have to pay dearly!'

And with these words, my new friend climbed proudly down the steps that led to the former Society for the Protection of Animals, filled with cheerful optimism. I followed him without really caring whether anyone might see us or not.

14

On the roof of
the coal shed

*In which black cats meet on the roof of a coal shed,
not knowing that they have been betrayed.*

The emergency meeting of the representatives of all black
cats of the island took place that same night. I had
placed all my hopes in this meeting. Fortunately, most black
cats I had informed had accepted my invitation. The roof
tiles were packed with them. There were delegates from all
quarters, all neighbourhoods, all back streets, alleys, lanes
and terraces. Lean and chubby, scrawny and well-fed,
domestic and stray. There were around eighty black cats in
total, maybe more. From a distance, it seemed as if the roof
of the shed had been laid with glittering emeralds – as so
many green eyes sparkled in the darkness.

I was the first to arrive, together with my mate, Choptail.
We chatted for a while, gave each other courage and when
everyone had arrived, I summed up the situation.

'My fellow felines,' I concluded, 'our necks are on the line. The Guardians of Good Luck are well-organised, well-connected and determined to wipe us out, down to the last whisker. If we don't act, if we don't react, if we don't find ways to counteract, they will have bumped us off in a matter of months, according to their plans, as I am informed.'

As soon as I had finished, Timothy Puttypuss, a well-fed cat from the northern suburbs, took the stand.

'I believe the situation is being somewhat exaggerated,' he said. 'Only a few people really believe such outrageous superstitions. Most people are sensible, decent and kind-hearted. They love and care for their cats. Consequently, I believe there is no need for undue anxiety.'

'What about the demonstrations? The posters? The public speeches? The arson attacks? Doesn't all this mean anything to you?' I protested. 'Let alone the fact that they have already drowned scores of cats! Why, cats are probably being drowned as we speak in the hamam from hell!'

'This is not my point. Of course we need to be careful. We must keep a watchful eye.'

'That is not enough!' I yelled, beside myself with anger.

'I'm sorry to interrupt,' spoke Nournour, who represented all spoiled house cats, in a timid voice. 'I have a rather important question to ask.'

'We're listening.'

'Can you eat the cuckoo from a cuckoo clock?'

'Has that got anything to do with our subject?' I asked, perplexed.

'Hasn't it?'

'No, it hasn't!'

'That's true,' admitted Nournour. 'But I have been seriously preoccupied with this question for quite some time now. What I mean is, if I ever manage to lay my paws on that shameless fowl that opens and closes the door and goes in and out of the clock, sneering and laughing at me, will I be able to eat it? Yes or no? Is it edible or isn't it and I'd be wasting my time as well as risking breaking a tooth? I don't want to repeat the fiasco with the rubber duck I fished out of the bathtub that was totally unchewable!'

'Listen, mate.' I put him in his place rather strictly. 'Can you please do us all a favour and forget all about the cuckoo that goes in and out and up and down and whatnot and try to concentrate on the subject at hand?'

'I will do my best!' Nournour promised.

'It is my firm belief that we must perform a serious and thorough study of the whole situation,' said Pickles, a grocer's cat who represented all grocers' cats and who stank of salted herrings. 'What I'm saying is that the proper thing is to set up a committee of distinguished black cats, who will assign the in-depth study of the subject in question to qualified sub-committees and then we will submit rationalised proposals to a local committee, which will consist of representatives of all the existing committees, who, in turn, will report their findings to a central committee.'

'Committees? Studies? Sub-committees?' yelled an indignant Choptail. 'Are you in your right mind, Pickles? We haven't got time to lose. We're lost if we don't act now!'

'I agree!' came Gary the Grabber's voice, to our salvation.

Gary the Grabber, otherwise known as Attila the Hug, was a dynamic one-whiskered tom cat from the west suburbs. When I say one-whiskered I mean that he only had whiskers on one side of his muzzle. They say that a jealous pussycat by the name of Clawthilde had pulled out those on the other side in a fit of passionate jealousy one fine January night.

'We haven't got time to waste,' continued Gary the Grabber decisively. 'To confront such an organised threat like this, we have to take immediate and determined action! And to achieve that we need a powerful, dynamic and inspired leader.'

He paused for a moment to draw breath and continued in the same commanding tone, 'I put forward myself as the leader.'

'I agree with the previous speaker,' jumped in Darren the Daring, the old soldier who was missing part of his right ear. 'He is absolutely right to maintain that we have no time to waste. I also agree one hundred per cent with his opinion that we need a powerful, dynamic and inspired leader. The only point which finds me in complete and total disagreement is that in my humble, but universally respected opinion, he is not the right type for our leader.'

'Is that so? Who is the right type, then?' asked Gary the Grabber gravely.

'Myself.'

'You? You as a leader? That's a good one! Forgive me if I snort!' Gary the Grabber laughed. 'If you see a beefy rat, your knees turn to jelly! Whereas I – I'm – I'm dynamic and charismatic. I'm smart and flexible. I've got prestige, I've got nerve and loquacity. Am I lacking in something? Nothing at all! I unanimously proclaim myself the leader of the campaign for the preservation of black cats! We won't be intimidated! We won't back down! We won't give in! We won't be destroyed! We will fight! We will resist! We will triumph and achieve great things!'

'Whoa! Time out! You're getting a bit ahead of yourself, don't you think? I won't take such cheap insults, especially when they come from a half-bully with half a set of whiskers!' grunted Darren the Daring with rage. 'You've got some cheek to say my knees turn to jelly, you rat turd!'

'Take your words back right now!' growled Gary the Grabber menacingly.

'You do it for me – if you've got the guts!'

A word here, a word there, and soon we had a full-blown spat on our hands. Gary the Grabber arched his back. Darren drew out his claws. I stood between them in an attempt to stop them.

'Cut it out, you two! Come to your senses! What on earth do you think you're doing, guys? The ship is sinking and all you do is fight each other? Have you gone completely mad? Don't you realise the seriousness of the situation?'

After things had cooled down a bit, the meeting resumed.

'It is my personal belief that we must leave this place,' said Flotsam, an old ship's cat who'd travelled for years and years before returning to the island to spend his old age in peace and quiet.

'Where should we go, then?' asked Choptail.

'To Siam, Ankara, the Thousand-canary Islands – somewhere, anywhere. We should organise a mass exodus. A flight. A run for our lives, in other words!'

'And leave our favourite haunts? No way!' declared Loma Paloma, a long-haired kitty who liked to wash all day long, and who represented the stray cats who had been adopted, and weren't strays any more.

'No one wants to give up their old haunts. No one wants to emigrate, but what else is there to do? It's the only solution!' Flotsam insisted.

'Sorry to interrupt again,' meowed Nournour the house cat, timidly, 'but could you clarify something for me, please? In these Thousand-canary Islands you were talking about earlier, are there any cuckoo clocks or just canary clocks?'

I gave him a look of reprimand and was about to tell him

off once more when Nostrilix, a tom cat with short thick fur, who represented the country cats, intervened. 'I have something very significant to say! Pay close attention if you please, so that you comprehend and can explain to me, if you will, what I think I'm about to say.'

Nostrilix meant well, but when he spoke in public he liked to sound important, and as a result, even he, himself, found it hard, sometimes, to understand precisely what he was talking about.

'It is true that the situation is critical,' he began. 'It is not crotical, nor is it cratical. It is critical. And it is criminal that it is critical because it would have been helpful if it were not critical. Consequently, if we are to resolve this resolution, we all need to be willing to present our point of view, the presentation of which will avert any transferral of responsibility and unmistakably proclaim our intention of pursuing the juxtaposition of the sequence of all potential possibilities, which enter into an unprecedented . . .'

I was about to cut in when I heard the barking. My fur stood on end. The others had heard it, too. Deadly silence descended on the roof of the coal shed.

As soon as we realised exactly what was going on, our blood froze. A whole pack of ravening wolfhounds had surrounded the block, snarling and raring to tear us to pieces. At the same time, around forty nightmarish shadows rose from the surrounding rooftops. They were the shadows of men carrying nets, torches, shotguns and spiked clubs. They made for us, growling with manic fury.

'Exterminate them!'

'Don't let a single one get away!'

'Beat the living daylights out of them!'

It was plain to see: we had been set up! Someone had squealed on us. A snitch had informed the Guardians of Good Luck of our meeting.

'We're surrounded!' I yelled, a new feeling of despair sweeping over me. What followed was horrible, abominable. Everyone was seized by unbelievable panic. Some cats attempted to run this way, some scampered that way, without the slightest hope of escape. Some tried to leap across to the rooftops opposite, and others, crazed with terror, charged about madly and got caught up in the nets that our persecutors had spread – or in their despair, plunged down to the street below, into the foaming mouths of the hounds whose sharp, white fangs glinted in the dark.

I could hear gunshots, obscene swearing, muffled wailing, brutal laughter, piercing screams and the pitiful laments of cats. I could hear gasps, hoarse cries and frenzied barking. My heart pounded with fear.

All of a sudden, a bullet whizzed past my ear. I saw Choptail hit by a club, flying through the air. I grabbed him with my teeth by the scruff of the neck and we disappeared down a chimney.

We landed on our backs, one on top of the other, amidst the cinders of a burnt-out furnace. I could still hear the yells and cries of the ongoing bloody assault on the roof. I shook the ashes off me. Choptail was lying on the floor, wounded, with blood trickling from his mouth, looking at me imploringly.

'Choptail! What have they done to you?'

'I think this is where I get off the bus!'

'What are you talking about? Don't say that! Have courage! You'll get over it, Choptail! You'll see! We'll go to the fish tavern again. We'll grab a dozen sea breams, heh? What do you say?'

'You go there yourself, mate, and remember your friend, the Sizzler!' He spoke with difficulty.

'Choptail! Sizzler! Commandocat! My friend! My mate! Don't die on me! I beg you, please, don't leave me like this!'

He tried to speak but couldn't.

'Talk to me, Mr Fry! Say something! Talk to me! Talk to me!'

'You know something?' he managed to say. 'It's not right . . .'

'What's not right?'

Speaking was hard work for him and the red patch of blood around him grew bigger and bigger. 'That black cats bring bad luck. The right thing to say is that . . . that . . .'

'What? What is the right thing to say?'

'That superstitious people bring bad luck to black cats,'

he gasped, short of breath.

And with these words his eyes closed, his head leaned slowly forward and he took his last breath right there, in front of my eyes.

I stood still for a while, looking at him. It was as if time had stopped. Then, slowly and softly, without knowing why, I started to sing his favourite song, like a lullaby, as if I was tucking him in for the night, as if I was saying goodbye . . .

> *I knew a cat called Abigail*
> *Who had such a lovely tail*
>
> *All the tom cats stood in line*
> *To date this lovely feline.*
> *They got the deepest thrill*
> *From her tail's dainty frill . . .*

I couldn't go on. There was a big lump in my throat.

Up above, on the roof, the frightening sounds of the assault had begun to die down.

15

A shooting star in the river

In which our hero meets a friend on a stone bridge over a deep, dark river, while a cat show is taking place in the park with the lilac trees.

Few of the cats who had met on the roof of the coal shed managed to survive the atrocious carnage that night. I was one of the lucky ones. I waited for the nightmare to die down, then licked my paws and neck clean of the blood and slipped out through a half-open window with broken glass panes and into what was now a deserted street.

I wandered about aimlessly. I refused to believe that all this had really happened, that we had been betrayed, we'd been decimated and, most painful of all, I had suddenly lost Choptail, my friend, my best mate.

A tangled web of thoughts weaved through my mind. Who had betrayed us? Who was to blame? Where would all this lead? Who would have ever thought that humans could be so inhuman . . . I walked as if I were lost, without taking any precautions, with untold sorrow gripping my heart.

I found myself among the tall trees of a shady park. The sweet smell of lilacs hung in the air. I could hear a brass band play a fanfare in the distance. 'Cat Show' said a banner stretched across the entrance to the park. Graziella came to my mind. The last time I saw her, she had mentioned something about taking part in some sort of beauty contest. I could hear applause. Could it be for her? I wondered. Was she just about to receive the first prize? Very possibly. She was so beautiful . . . I felt the need to see her again . . . I was just about to enter the park, but I changed my mind at the last moment. What was the point, any more? Filled with sorrow, I went on my way.

At some point, I realised that I had arrived at a stone bridge with three bow-shaped arches over a dark river. I climbed on to the parapet and silently watched the flow of the murky waters for a long time. It was as if they were whispering something to me, as if they were inviting me.

'Come!' they said. 'Come!'

I bent forward. I could see the sparkle of my eyes reflected on the gloomy surface. It appeared to me I was already deep in the water, looking at myself from the bottom of the river. I balanced on the edge. I imagined I was a ship's cat on the immense ocean, that I was on the windswept deck of a Spanish schooner that travelled to exotic places, laden with silk, gems and spices, and that all around me raged a terrible storm. The gigantic waves would swallow me, I would vanish in the silent depths for ever. What a heroic death for a much-travelled ship's cat . . .

'Don't tell me you've got the blues?' a voice was heard to say.

It was Tarmac. What the blazes was he doing here at this time of day?

'Say . . . What exactly are you trying to do there?' he asked, and it was as plain as day that he had picked up my intentions.

'It is none of your business!'

'Not planning to take a one-way dive, I hope?'

'Leave me alone, please. Do me a favour. I'm in no mood for conversation right now. I'd like to be left alone.'

'If you want to be left alone on the edge of the bridge, that's fine by me. But your lying alone at the bottom of the river does not strike me as a very good idea.'

'If only you knew . . .' I whispered. 'If only you knew.'

'What happened?'

'Something . . . something you can't begin to imagine.'

'Where? When?'

'A little while ago. On the roof of the coal shed.'

'Didn't the meeting go well?'

'Didn't it go well?' I gave a bitter laugh. 'They set us up, Tarmac. They killed who knows how many cats, without mercy, without reason or rhyme. I lost Choptail, my best mate. I lost my courage – I lost my faith in humanity. I've lost everything. Even my purrcious . . . Enough is enough. Goodbye.'

And with these words I jumped into the murky waters, or rather, I almost jumped, because Tarmac caught me by the scruff of the neck just in time. He looked me in the eyes.

'Choptail wouldn't have wanted you to go like that.'

'What would he have wanted?'

'He'd have wanted you to live. To save your own hide. To remember him. To avenge his untimely death. To save others if you can. As many as you can.'

'But what can I do, Tarmac? Tell me! What can I do on my own?'

'You're not alone. When one cat is in danger, all cats are. When one cat is threatened, they all are. Black or white, grey or ginger. Whatever their colour may be, whatever their breed!'

There was truth in what he said and his words gave me back my courage. We started to talk. We sat at the stone parapet of the bridge and talked for a long time. I told him about my heartache; he told me about his. Until recently, he'd lived in a house with a lovely little girl with dimples on her cheeks, who literally adored him. Her name was Marilena. She fed him a thousand delicacies, she held him in her arms, she made him little balls out of tin foil to play with. Her parents, though, had thrown him out when the great persecution began; despite Marilena's bitter tears, despite her pleas to let him hide somewhere so that he would stay safe.

A shooting star plunged into the river in a shower of sparkles. I remembered the twinkle in the eyes of my late mate, Choptail.

'I made a wish,' Tarmac confessed.

'What kind of wish?'

'To see Marilena once again. I miss this girl. You don't know how much I miss her. They say that if you make a wish when you see a falling star, it will come true.'

'I hope they do, mate,' I said. 'I hope they do. I wish you and your Marilena are reunited, one fine day.'

'If you need me, you'll find me at Mother Reene's soup kitchen,' he said before we parted. 'That's where I'll be, around midday.'

16

Mother Reene feeds her friends

In which a kind-hearted old woman feeds hungry cats in a poor neighbourhood and our hero witnesses the torture of a cuddly cat.

Over the following days things went from bad to worse. Our enemies multiplied. So did the dangers. Black cats became fewer and fewer. We simply had to find the way and the means to protect ourselves. Then I remembered Tarmac's words: 'When one cat is in danger, all cats are. When one cat is threatened, they all are.' Whichever way I thought about it, I knew that he was right. We had to mobilise all cats: white, grey, ginger or brown, tabby, tortoiseshell or piebald. We had to persuade all cats, no matter what their colour, to join forces with us.

I decided to find Tarmac and ask him to put into practice the idea his words had given me. Now that Darren the Daring, Gary the Grabber and all the other cats with the makings of a leader were no longer among us, someone had to take the initiative before we were completely wiped out.

I knew where to look for Tarmac. As he'd said, like many other cats, he used to hang out in a plot of land behind a car graveyard, in a poor neighbourhood, where Mother Reene, a kind-hearted old woman with a lined face and a limp in her right leg, used to show up every day at noon, come rain or shine, bearing a big canvas bag with faded purple stripes, and feed the stray cats of the area fish-heads, fish-tails and any other scraps she could find.

'Here kitty-kitty! Here kitty!' she would call and lo and behold, dozens of cats would spring up from everywhere, behind the discarded armchairs with their stuffing hanging out, the gutted mattresses, the broken bathtubs and the shacks with the rusty sheet-irons, and rub their heads against her legs, meowing impatiently, accepting her offerings with grateful purrs.

Most humans considered Mother Reene to be half mad and smiled condescendingly when they saw her feed the cats. We were grateful to her, though. We weren't quite sure what else she did in her life. It was rumoured that she had lost her husband and her children in the big earthquake which had hit the island and then she had lost her mind, too. As far as I knew, she used to sell tangerines in the street market, some time ago. I'd seen her once cry out:

'Get your tangerines
From ol' Mother Reene's.'

Then again, she had worked as a cleaning lady in the public toilets. To us, though, Mother Reene wasn't the lowly toilet cleaner or the mad old woman – she was a fairy godmother who cared for and pampered stray cats with no personal gain. How many times, when I was starving, hadn't I accepted her offer with immense gratitude? She was the only human who had a perfect understanding of our language, who knew how we felt, what we were saying, what we were thinking and shared our worries and our fears.

'Mum, why are black cats so bad?' I heard a child ask his mother as I was sneaking through the vegetable market.

'Don't you ever use that language again!' she answered angrily and smacked him. 'If I ever hear you use the words "black cat" again, I'll put black pepper in your mouth. Is that clear, you wicked boy?'

'Oh, all right! I won't say black cat again,' said the child sulkily.

I walked on. A few metres down the road, I saw a young couple get off a coach drawn by two chestnut horses and then go into a flower shop. The coachman jumped from his seat and started tightening the harnesses on the horses' sides. He was wearing tall, tan boots and carried a horse-whip under his arm.

The flowers at the entrance to the flower shop gave off a sweet smell. The shop's errand boy was sprinkling them with water from a bucket. A couple of bees buzzed round a can of chrysanthemums. Then I saw a black cat come out of a sidestreet and approach the coachman. I recognised him immediately. It was Purrcy. He went up to the coachman and rubbed himself against his boots, purring like a steam engine. The coachman gave him a hard kick in the ribs and a stunned Purrcy ended up lying on his back on the pavement, five feet away. The horses snorted restlessly. Purrcy turned over, got up and was about to leave, puzzled over the unexpected kick, when the coachman, white with rage, approached the cat, raised his horse-whip furiously and brought it down on him with force, without pity, again and again, ignoring Purrcy's desperate cries. I saw the poor animal writhe with pain and turn his bloody muzzle imploringly towards his attacker, as if begging for mercy, but the man went on flogging him savagely until Purrcy moved no more. He had paid very dearly for his trusting nature and his yearning for some petting.

The coachman with the tan boots climbed back on to his bench, red faced. I waited for a moment for the coach to disappear so I could run to Purrcy's help, when suddenly a lady with a canary-yellow, broad-brimmed hat and a shiny strawberry-coloured purse stormed out of the flower shop, screaming and pointing at me.

'That's him! That's the cat who attacked me the other day! He's responsible for all those accidents! He's the villain who tried to murder me! He's the reason why the kiosk owner had a nervous breakdown and that priceless Chinese vase was shattered to smithereens!'

I vanished into thin air. Life was becoming impossible. How had we come to this? A new danger lay in wait with every single step I took. I decided once more to follow more secluded paths. So, taking a shortcut through gardens and orchards, jumping over walls, fences and ditches, climbing over roofs, porches and railings, I finally reached the plot where Mother Reene, cheerful as always, with a threadbare shawl thrown over her shoulders, was feeding a multi-coloured crowd of cats table scraps and fish heads. The symphony of meowing was enough to blow your ears off.

I took my share, too and when lunch was over, I approached Tarmac and told him of the plan I had in mind. He was glad to see me and eager to offer his help to put the plan into action as soon as possible. We asked any other cats who happened to be there to notify all the cat population of an emergency meeting, the following night, round the chimney of the Gourmandeur and Co. chocolate factory.

When night fell, I returned to the pavement outside the flower shop and looked for Purrcy, but he wasn't there. Apparently, his body had been removed. I picked up a wilted

chrysanthemum that had fallen out of one of the cans of the
flower shop and placed it on the spot where the cuddliest cat
on the island had drawn his last breath.

17

Shorty shows up again

*In which two suspicious characters conspire, a cat
pays dearly for a few mouthfuls of canned tuna and
the park keepers fish a dead swan out of the pond.*

The following morning my stomach rattled like a
drum. I was so hungry I couldn't see straight. Doing the
rounds in the rubbish bins was out of the question, because
the Guardians had set up volunteer groups that lay in wait,
hidden behind them, knowing very well it was where hungry
cats hang out. You went there, unsuspecting, to dig out a
fishbone for breakfast and got a thump on the head with a
heavy club, instead.

So I decided to take a walk in the park, hoping to
stumble upon something edible to stop my tummy
rumbling. I knew that sometimes the young couples who had
a picnic on the cool, deep-green grass under the willows,
were too occupied with exchanging kisses and carving little
hearts on the bark of the trees to notice what was going on

around them. Other visitors, who were – how shall I put it? – more advanced in years, tended to need their forty winks after a good meal and if you were lucky, you could end up with a whole whitebait or half a cupcake before they even knew you had been there.

I picked one of the more secluded areas of the park and summoned my sense of smell, hoping that soon the irresistible aroma of tinned tuna or, even better, salmon, would tease my nostrils. Instead of the desired scents, though, I smelled something else. It was an unpleasant smell. A smell that punched me on the nose. Iodine and mint.

I followed the smell and a bit further down, on a bench that was out of the way, near a bed of tulips, I spotted the back of the short man with the greasy cap. I approached silently from behind. There was somebody else sitting next to him. I couldn't see his face. I noticed, however, that he was wearing a fur coat and a fur hat. They spoke quietly, as if they were anxious not to be overheard. In the background, an elderly man was feeding peanuts to a squirrel and a few feet away a young mother was running after a plump toddler who came tumbling down every few steps or so.

'What you are asking of me, Monsieur Rapacine, is a touch difficult!' said Shorty. 'I could indulge you once or twice, for a fair price, naturally, but no more than that.'

'It's in your best interests to do it!' the other tried

to persuade him, in a voice that sounded like a rotten apple plunging into the sludgy waters of a sewer.

'The Guardians of Good Luck give me a good price, Monsieur Rapacine!'

'I'll pay even better. Ten a piece!'

'But what are you talking about? Who do you take me for? My conscience would never allow me to do such a thing! Poor cats . . . I don't say I'm against bumping them off but not like that. Not this way!'

'Twenty?'

'Twenty what?'

'Twenty a piece. Would your conscience give you permission, then?'

'Not quite, but for fifty an exception could be made . . . I'll have horrible pangs of remorse, but I'll grin and bear it.'

'Fifty? Are you insane?'

'Think of the profit!'

'So be it. You're skinning me alive, but I have no choice. I accept.'

'Bless your kind heart, Monsieur Rapacine. I'll let you know when I'm ready.'

'I'm counting on you. And don't breathe a word, right?'

'But of course, Monsieur Rapacine! D'you think I'm off my rocker? If anyone gets wind of what we're doing I'll be the first to cop it. Are you sure no one will be able to hear the screams?'

'Absolutely. The cellars are too deep in the ground and they're very well insulated. They can wail and howl as much as they like, for all I care. No one will be able to hear them! Oh, and there's something else, too. It's better if you don't come to me. I'll send the dwarves to collect the stuff.'

'All right but . . . they're quite grim, those dwarves. I get a chill down my spine every time I see them.'

'It goes with the job, I'm afraid. I can't say they don't enjoy torturing the little beasts – it makes their job a little less boring. It spices it up, so to speak. Besides the fact that the quality of the product is highly improved this way.'

What were they talking about? What had Shorty agreed to do for a price? What more horrible things could happen to cats besides what was already going on? What sort of dealings did these two have?

I strained my ears but did not hear anything that could have enlightened me.

The short man with the cap took a landing-net and a sack that lay beside him on the ground and got to his feet.

'I'm leaving first!' he said. 'We shouldn't be seen together.'

'Quite right. I'll stay here for about ten minutes and then I'm off. Cheerio!'

Shorty did not move. 'You forgot something, Monsieur Rapacine.'

'What?'

'The down payment.'

'What down payment? We said nothing about a down payment.'

'Ah, what's fair's fair! No down payment, no deal!'

'If that's the case, so be it. They say I skin my victims but you're worse. How much?'

'As much as you like as long as it's over a thousand.'

'All right! But if it ever occurs to you to double-cross me, you should have no doubts about your fate! I'll send the dwarves to give you the same treatment they are reserving for the cats!'

'You shouldn't say that Monsieur Rapacine, I get goosebumps!'

The stranger, whose face I had not seen yet, did not speak. He took out a thick snakeskin wallet and counted several greasy banknotes. The short man shoved them in his pocket and left.

I knew what risk I was taking, but I decided to follow him to find out where he was going. Luckily, Rapacine had unfolded a newspaper and was so engrossed in it that there was no fear that he might detect my presence.

All of a sudden, as I was ducking and weaving my way with every precaution on Shorty's trail, the smell I had so longed for teased my nostrils: tinned tuna. A few feet away, there was a young couple, a blonde girl with a pony-tail and a checked skirt and a clean-shaven young man with the first two buttons of his shirt undone. They were kissing and cuddling. Right in front of them there was a picnic blanket with a thermos flask, two egg cups, a few peaches and various other delicacies, among which was an open tin of tuna. Unfortunately, it had company, too. Somebody's muzzle was deep into the green and yellow tin. It belonged to a black cat who had made a start before me and, taking advantage of the young couple's embraces, was blissfully sampling the delicious contents of the tin. Immersed as he was in his tasty meal, though, he did not detect the presence of the short man with the cap who, like me, had noticed what was going on and had stealthily approached him from behind. And then, right there, in front of my eyes, with an expert move, the short man with the cap trapped the black cat in his net!

The young couple were highly amused by the sight.

The desperate cat was twisting and turning in the net, begging, 'Have mercy on me, kind sir! Please let me go! I'm not completely black, you see! I've got a pea-sized white spot. You can't see it right now, but it's behind my right ear . . . Please have mercy . . . I'm not completely and utterly black . . . If you let me go, I'll show you where real black cats are hiding. There's one now! Right there, behind you!'

Shorty turned round to see but I had already hidden behind a rubbish bin. Insensitive to his victim's pleas, he gave him a jab with a syringe and the meowing stopped at once. He shoved the cat in his sack and went on his way.

I was about to start following him again when I heard

loud voices and saw a crowd gathering quickly round the pond in the park. I climbed up a thick plane tree and peered down through the leaves. It was a strange sight. I saw two of the keepers pull a dead swan out of the pond. That was odd. Who could have killed it?

After the crowd had moved away and I was able to jump from the tree, the short man with the cap had vanished. I looked for the man he had been talking to, whose voice sounded like a rotten apple plunging into a sewer, but he was also gone. These were mysterious goings-on . . . Very mysterious.

18

The two chimney sweeps

In which cats of other colours seem reluctant to help black cats and our hero dunks his blazing tail into a barrelful of water.

When night fell, about a dozen cats of all colours, shades and shapes gathered together round the chimneys of the Gourmandeur and Co. chocolate factory.

Cinders and Ashley represented grey cats. Cottontail and Snowflake were the white cats' delegates. Cappuccino and Cinnamon stood in for brown and ginger cats. Cats of mixed or indeterminable colour were represented by Purripurr and Patches. Finally, Tarmac and myself represented – who else? – the few remaining black cats.

After we had finished the introductions, I brought the company up to date with the latest developments, which was not really necessary, since most of them had already found out what had happened from various other sources. Then I explained in detail the plans of the Guardians of Good

Luck and informed them of their contacts with top-ranking members of the government and other agents. I spoke with passion and emotion. I was almost desperate.

'My fellow cats. Our situation is critical! To go further, I would say it is hopeless. We need your urgent and unreserved support.'

'Do explain, exactly how do you think we can contribute?' Ashley wanted to know.

'The least you can do is to help us as much as you can.'

'How do you mean?'

'You could inform us of enemy moves,' explained Tarmac. 'Bring food secretly to our hiding places, because we can't move freely, and, generally, aid us in any and all ways.'

'But, dear friend, hold on a minute. If we do as you say, we run the risk of being considered your accomplices!' Cottontail pointed out.

'Accomplices in what?'

'In the bad luck you bring!'

'But we *don't* bring anyone bad luck! We've got nothing to do with bad luck! What are you talking about, Cottontail?'

'Obviously, I mean the bad luck that your detractors erroneously maintain that you bring about. Personally, I don't believe any of these unfounded accusations, you know, that whoever hangs out with you catches *jinxitis gravis*, which is highly contagious and absolutely lethal, otherwise I wouldn't be here with you – but would you move over a bit, mate, just to be on the safe side?'

I was on the point of giving him a piece of my mind, but I decided to let it pass and moved back a little.

'Your support is essential to us! We need every scrap of help you can offer.' Tarmac tried to persuade them once again. 'The Guardians of Good Luck aren't joking! They literally intend to annihilate us. They're bent on leaving not even one black cat alive on the island, not one!'

'We totally disagree with what the Guardians stand for and unreservedly condemn their abhorrent policy!' Snowflake reassured me.

'We feel an immense sympathy for your lot,' agreed Cottontail. 'Believe me when I say that your problems are our own, too!'

These statements pleased me, but not for long.

'But then – how shall I put it –' Cottontail concluded his thought. 'We couldn't possibly jeopardise our own safety, trying to ensure yours. Otherwise, these lunatics may start harassing us as well and then where will we be?'

I tried hard to contain my rage. 'What is it that you are saying? Are you going to deny us the help we need so badly? Are you going to abandon us and let us cope as best we can? Why are you doing this? For heaven's sake, comrades, aren't we all cats? What does it matter that we happen to be of a different colour?'

'Hold it, mate!' was Cottontail's indignant reply. 'Don't

you put words in my mouth! This is really too much. If you didn't hear what I said, I'll repeat it for you: we're willing to offer any possible help!'

'But how?' I asked him to explain, with new hope. 'How are you going to do that, Cottontail?'

'Mentally.'

'What do you mean "mentally"?'

'I mean that our thoughts will be by your side in the fight for your just cause. As for the rest, we want no involvement!'

'I agree and approve!' meowed Snowflake. 'I don't see why we white cats should put our necks on the line for your sakes! What have we got to gain?'

I must confess that I'd never expected such a selfish response.

'What about you, Cinders? What have you got to say?' I asked. I had known Cinders for years and, in the old times, we had spent whole nights on the roof tiles together, serenading pretty pussies, so I hoped that he might see things from a different, less selfish perspective.

'Who, me?' Cinders' mind had been wandering. Lying flat on his belly, with his head between his front paws, he was watching with interest a ladybird that was climbing slowly on one of the chimneys of the chocolate factory.

'Yes, you!'

'Erm . . . ah . . .' He hummed and hawed. 'You see we – that is grey cats – we most definitely have every good intention of supporting you, but if we ever attempt to do that, just because of the fact that we are grey, you understand, there might be a chance that we are mistaken for black cats ourselves and get into trouble too, heaven forbid. So all in all, I think it's best to avoid any such pitfalls. Therefore, I am of the opinion that it is white cats that should help you, as no one will ever suspect them and, in their case, there is no danger of confusion! Er . . . That's all I have to say!'

'You always know how to get yourself out of tight spots, don't you?' said Cottontail, vexed.

'What's your position?' I asked Cinnamon, a cat with eyes the colour of honey and a long, supple tail that, rumour had it, she could twist into a knot.

'The ginger cats of this island happen to be greatly outnumbered by black and white cats,' Cinnamon stated. 'It is therefore our duty to take good care of ourselves. Besides, what could we poor kitties do, seeing that there are so few of us?'

'And anyway, the whole matter is not something that concerns us directly!' added Cappuccino, a brown tabby who had a thing about personal hygiene, and went on cleaning himself with his tongue.

The sun was setting. I pinned my last hopes on Patches and Purripurr.

'Personally, I believe that you deserve every help and support in your just cause,' Purripurr addressed the company. He was a grey and ginger cat with orange and cream stripes, one green eye, one blue and a tail the colour of maize.

'But as you may well understand,' added Patches, a ginger cat with cinnamon and dark burgundy patches, violet eyes and a khaki-yellow tail, who also went by the name Pot-pourri, 'we cannot possibly take any final decisions on our own at this very moment.'

'Why's that?'

'We must consult cats of all other shades and colour combinations.'

'And who are they?'

'White cats with black stripes, grey cats with ginger stripes, brown tabbies with lilac ears, black cats with yellow tails, cream-coloured cats with ginger flashes, red cats with grey ears, Siamese cats with –'

'When are you planning to consult all these cats?' I cut him short impatiently.

'Why, as soon as possible!' was Patches' vague reply.

'When is that, to be exact?'

'I trust that in a couple of months we will have the collected opinions of all 1,225 varieties of cats of mixed colour and be in a position to give a more definitive answer.'

'But, in a couple of months there won't even be a black whisker left, let alone a black cat!' Tarmac yelled at him. 'In a couple of months black cats will be no more!'

'In such a case, we will make every effort to speed up the consultation procedure, but we cannot, of course, guarantee that it will yield results in the near future!' claimed Purripurr.

'So, to sum it up, you are abandoning us to the mercy of all those maniacs?'

'But of course not! Our thoughts and good wishes will accompany you in your arduous fight!' Cottontail reassured me once again.

'To hell with your thoughts, and to double hell with your good wishes!' I burst out.

'Let me tell you, mate!' said Cottontail with rage. 'Enough is enough! I have not come here to be insulted by a bunch of vulgar alley cats! I'm in enough danger already by participating in this unlawful meeting. I'm risking my neck for you and this is what I get by way of thanks. And I'm not even mentioning the dead swans . . .'

'What have the dead swans got to do with our case?'

'Yeah, yeah! As if we didn't know what's going on . . . Leave it . . . it's best if we let sleeping dogs lie. In any case, seeing that no one appreciates my good intentions, I'm leaving!' declared Cottontail.

'Me, too!' decided Snowflake. 'What ingratitude, by Bastet! What terrible ingratitude . . .' She clicked her tongue. 'What is the world coming to?'

'Wait! Where are you going? I didn't mean to hurt your feelings!' I ran after them. It was no use. They both left with their tails stuck up high in the air and an air of wounded dignity.

When I returned to our meeting place, the only cat I found waiting for me was Tarmac. The others had grabbed the opportunity to leg it, too.

The setting sun bathed the roof of the chocolate factory in rich gold and purple hues. The sky had taken a rosy hue with red and violet highlights. The ladybird had almost reached the top of the chimney.

'We should have expected this!' Tarmac meowed stoically. 'It's no use, no one is prepared to risk their neck for our sakes.'

'Say, Tarmac, what did Cottontail mean when he mentioned the dead swans?'

'How should I know? One thing's for sure. We can't expect any real help from their lot. When the going gets tough, they go the other way.'

'But why? Why such sheer indifference?'

'They're scared stiff. Not to mention the fact that they've got a vested interest.'

'What do you mean?'

'No one said it in so many words, but it's not that difficult to figure it out.'

'Figure out what?'

'Fewer cats equals more mice, fish-heads and rubbish-bin delicacies per head for those that remain. In other words, the per capita rubbish is on the increase.'

'So, the bottom line is that we've got to do what we've got to do expecting no help whatsoever –'

My speech was cut short because, at that very moment, from behind the chimney with the ladybird, appeared a chimney sweep. His chin was stubbly. His eyes were vacant. He held a jerry can full of petrol.

I had barely managed to recover from the shock, when I saw a second chimney sweep with a thick neck pop up from behind the shadow of another chimney. His hair was dishevelled. His malevolent grin revealed two broken teeth. He was carrying a few balls of greyish cotton wool and a huge yellow matchbox.

With a brutish laugh that distorted his face, the first chimney sweep expertly tossed the contents of the can towards us, soaking us in petrol, while the second started to set fire to the cotton bits one by one and throw the flaming balls straight at us.

'They're trying to burn us alive!' I hear Tarmac's voice. 'Run!'

He didn't have to tell me twice! With a swift manoeuvre, I slip between the first chimney sweep's legs. He stumbles, swearing at me. Just when I think I'm out of it, I am forced to make an about-turn because three more chimney sweeps appear in front of me, bearing jerry cans with petrol, cotton balls and matches, as well. I retreat and at the same time realise we're surrounded. Some are sprinkling us with petrol, while others, with horrific grins, are throwing lit matches and flaming cotton balls, one after the other. One of them lands on my tail, which goes up in flames immediately.

With a heart-rending meow, I do something I would never have attempted had I not found myself in such an emergency. I fling myself into the air, jump off the roof and land in a barrel full of rainwater, which stands on the pavement, next to a drainpipe. I go all the way down to the bottom of the barrel – almost drown – but I hold my breath. I imagine that I am a veteran ship's cat battling with the raging sea to keep up my courage, come up to the surface, give my body an almighty push, hang on to the wooden rim with my claws, struggle out of the barrel and – dripping wet – make myself scarce.

'Are you OK?' I hear Tarmac's voice panting over my shoulder.

'You go the other way!' I yell at him, running. 'Turn right there! If they're after us, it's best if we split.'

'Did you burn your tail?'

'Just a bit. It's OK, really! Only a little singe. Run for it!' I say. 'Go!'

19

The secret lab

*In which a black cat steals a lump of sugar and claims
to have discovered a life-saving formula.*

Tarmac turned into a narrow alley and I went on running on my own. I tore down a sloping road, sped past a group of laughing children who were kicking a rag-ball, ran across the square with the statue of a knight on horseback, climbed up a telegraph pole and, from there, jumped on to a brick wall that was about two metres tall. Finally, I stopped for a while to catch my breath.

Then I saw another black cat come out of a nearby grocer's with a lump of sugar between his teeth. Hot on his heels, there came a flushed, panting grocer, wearing a greasy apron; behind him were three errand boys brandishing an assortment of brooms and feather dusters. The grocer, who was clutching a big clay pot, dipped his hand in it and threw handfuls of huge green olives at the catapulting cat.

'Here's one for you, you thief! And there's another one!' he shouted.

I had to intervene. My fellow cat was in urgent need of some brotherly help. With a dive that would have made a goalkeeper proud, I plunged between the legs of the raging grocer who lost his balance and slipped. The pot flew in the air and its contents spilled on to the pavement. The errand boys who followed skidded on the slippery olives and performed a few pirouettes in the air before they found themselves lying on their backs, a few metres away, among the upturned crates of a greengrocer's stand, garnished from top to bottom with aubergines, broccoli and string beans.

'A thousand thanks, mate!' said the panting cat to me when we stopped running a while later. 'Let me introduce myself – Federico Firenze, alchemist and inventor of world-shaking inventions. You are surely wondering where I am running to with this cube of sugar I have purloined from the grocer's.'

'That's exactly what I'm doing!'

'Then follow me, my friend, and you will not regret it.'

The words of the strange cat had excited my curiosity, so I followed him without hesitation.

'You lucky devil,' he said, as he turned first left, then right, into the weaving streets of an unfamiliar neighbour-hood with gloomy buildings. 'It's your lucky day, today. A good turn deserves another. You helped me lose the grocer and his errand boys so you deserve to learn a closely guarded secret.'

He led the way behind a lumber-mill to a derelict building with wooden balconies that were on the verge of collapsing – and there he suddenly vanished.

'Federico, what's going on? Where are you?' I said, worried.

I saw him peep out from a long, narrow window with hazy, broken glass panes and cracks that spread like huge spider's webs. 'This way!' he beckoned.

I slipped through a broken glass pane and found myself in a stone-walled basement covered with cobwebs. In one of the corners stood an open trunk, brimming with rusty keys, tarnished bicycle bells and grimy hands from alarm clocks. Next to it were stacks of old Chinese dictionaries, atlases with crumbling bindings, yellowing almanacs, broken rattles and a wicker hamper in which I could just make out a tattered old conjuror's hat and a bridal veil, half-buried in grains of rice, peppercorns and mothballs. On the other side of the basement stood an oblong-shaped, worm-eaten work bench, littered with test tubes, dusty scales, gyroscopes, little phials, graters, pestles and mortars, tweezers, pipettes and various other odd tools and instruments, some of which I had never seen before. There was also a small clay basin with white liquid and a pair of brass scales, with a coconut cut in half on one pan and on the other, thin, white lengths of thread, three blue beads against the evil eye and a piece of chalk.

'What do you think of my secret lab?' asked Federico proudly as he deposited the cube of sugar on to a tea saucer.

'It's rather dusty!' I said, sneezing two or three times in succession.

One of the spiders that was weaving its web in one corner stopped to register its annoyance and then went on with its work.

'I'm inspired by dust,' bragged Federico. 'The dustier the environment, the more successful my inventions! It is here, my friend, in this humble basement laboratory, that, within a few minutes, the greatest invention of the century will take place.'

'What do you mean?'

'I'll explain. In the meantime, would you be so kind as to stir the contents of this bowl, here.'

I dipped my paw into the white liquid and, as I stirred, listened to Federico speak with interest.

'Can you tell me,' he asked, 'why people persecute us, and by "us" I mean not just you and me but all black cats?'

'Because we're black.'

'What is the solution, therefore?'

'Run faster and don't let them catch us?'

'No! That's only a temporary solution. I want you to tell me what the permanent solution is!'

'I don't know. What is it?'

'Change colour.'

'Change *what*?'

'Colour. Become white.'

'Are you all there?'

'Of course I am. If we become white, they will have no reason to persecute us. Isn't that right?'

I looked at him, puzzled. 'And how do you suggest that we do that?'

'Incredible as it may seem, I have invented the formula for turning black into white!'

'Are you sure?'

'Of course I am. I understand that you may find it difficult to believe me, but I assure you that I have cracked it. Would you like to know what the ingredients are?'

'If it's not too much trouble.'

'They're seven in total. And I've got all seven of them here, in my secret lab. Are you following me? It's history in the making, right here, right now.'

'I'm following,' I assured him, without having decided whether I was dealing with a crackpot, a cretin or a crook.

'Do you know what the stuff you're stirring in that bowl is?' he asked.

'What?'

'Coconut milk. That's the first ingredient.'

'What's the second?'

'Dewdrops from the cups of arum lilies. Hmm ... Where did I put them? Let me see . . . Ah, here they are!'

Federico picked out a cut-glass phial, pulled out the stopper and added three drops of lily-dew to the bowl with the coconut milk.

'The third ingredient is the white from a white dove's first egg!' he continued.

And with these words, he took a dove's egg out of a tiny egg cup, broke it expertly in half and emptied the white into the bowl with the coconut milk and the lily-dew.

'Excellent!' he muttered to himself with satisfaction. 'And now for the fourth ingredient. Hmmm ... What is the fourth ingredient? Ah, yes. A lump of sugar. Can you see it anywhere? Where did I put it?'

'It's right there! On the saucer! Inside the parrot cage.'

Federico carefully picked up the cube of sugar and dropped it into the bowl with the coconut milk, the lily-dew and the white of the dove's egg.

'Splendid,' he said, 'splendid ... And now, the fifth ingredient.'

'What's the fifth ingredient?'

'Water from a melted snowman.'

Speechless, I watched him take a tin cup that stood between an abacus and a candlestick, and let a few drops of the water from a melted snowman fall into the bowl with the coconut milk, the lily-dew, the white of the dove's egg and the lump of sugar, which had dissolved by now.

'The great moment is near,' he said. 'It's time to add the

sixth ingredient to the mixture.'

'What's the sixth ingredient?'

'A pinch of grated chalk. There it is! On the scales! I stole it from the classroom while the children were doing their gymnastics in the schoolyard!'

He grated it and added a pinch of the powdered chalk to the bowl with the coconut milk, the lily-dew, the white of the dove's egg, the lump of sugar and the water from a melted snowman.

'And now, all that is left is the last ingredient. Three lengths of thread from a bridal veil. Here they are. I've got them.' He took the white thread from the scales.

'Where did you get them?' I asked.

'It's a long story – I grabbed the bridal veil while the bride was taking a shower, before she got dressed for the wedding. As I was trying to get out, the rest of the bridal dress fell over me and before I could disentangle myself I had ripped it to shreds with my little nails. The poor girl had to get married in her bathrobe, but what can you do? It was all in the cause of science. You can't have inventions without sacrifices,' Federico said, and carefully added the three pieces of thread from the bridal veil to the bowl with the coconut milk, the lily-dew, the white of the dove's egg, the lump of sugar, the water from a melted snowman and the chalk powder.

'What do we do now?' I asked, stirring all the time.

'Now, we'll say the magic words.'

'What are the magic words?'

'These!'

Federico bent over the basin and chanted, evocatively, three times . . .

> *'Potion – make all black cats turn white*
> *Make a bright day of the darkest night.*
> *Potion – make all cats look right*
> *Turn their fur from black to light.'*

I had lost all track of time by now and suddenly noticed we were in the depths of the night. Moonbeams slipped through the dusty window and painted the cobwebby walls of the basement with silvery hues.

'Splendid,' said Federico.

'What's going to happen, now?'

'What do you think? I'll take one sip and I'll become white.'

He lowered his face into the basin and took a good sip. Then he looked at me with eyes that shone with excitement. 'As I haven't got a mirror to hand, would you be so good as to let me know when I start getting whiter . . . All right?'

'Yeah, right,' I assured him.

'Are you watching me?'

'Yes, I am.'

'Carefully?'

'You can't get more careful than this.'

'It may start with my ear, my tail or my muzzle. You never know . . .'

My eyes were fixed on him but I could see no difference in the colour of his muzzle, his tail or his ears.

'What's happening?' he asked, ten minutes later. 'Am I turning white? Am I?'

'No.'

'Not at all?'

'Not at all.'

'It can't be . . . Are you sure?'

'Yes, I am.'

'Are you short-sighted, by any chance?'

'No.'

'Long-sighted?'

'Nope.'

'Colour blind?'

'My eyes are just fine.'

A couple of hours went by, but Federico remained as black as coal.

'Federico . . . I think you're wasting your time,' I said in a friendly tone.

'Not so fast! You can't rush things! Do you think it's that easy for a black cat to become white? Hang on a little longer! Let's wait until daybreak, at least! Just try not to fall asleep, though, and miss the sensational moment of the transformation.'

I spent all night watching Federico and so did he! He stayed up all night looking me in the eyes, waiting to see them widen with surprise, rapture and admiration.

'Ahem . . . You know something?' he finally said around daybreak. 'Maybe I shouldn't have drunk it.'

'Yeah, maybe you should have bathed in it!'

'You might be right! Or maybe I should have coated my fur with the mixture. I'll dunk my tail in and see if it becomes white.'

He dunked his tail in but it did not become white.

'Look,' I said to him, 'I'm sorry to say it again but I think you're wasting your time.'

'You're really mistrustful, aren't you? My formula is infallible. There must have been something wrong with one of the minor details. Maybe I should have added more dewdrops, or maybe I should have got a bigger dove's egg . . . Then, maybe those who say that swans' are the only solution are right. I can't be that far off. I'll get there. And then I'll sell the recipe to black cats and become fabulously rich.'

'I should be going, really.'

'That's fine . . . You can come by in a week or so, if you like. Maybe I'll have cracked it by then.'

I left him thoughtfully scrutinising his tail and went out into the street.

20
Under the tub

In which our hero hides in a laundry room and meets an old acquaintance.

Would I really want to change colour, if I could? I asked myself as I walked through the narrow streets of the strange, run-down neighbourhood. And, if I managed it, would I still be the same me or would somebody else be myself?

As I was passing by a courtyard with a thick, shady climbing vine, a toddler who was weeing in a tin pot saw me and started to jump up and down, spraying the immediate surroundings and yelling at full blast: 'Mummy! Mummyyyy . . . Back gat! Back gat!'

The aforementioned mummy, who was wearing a flowery dressing-gown with turned-up sleeves and who was hanging babygros and bibs out on a line to dry, heard the squeaky squeals of her darling little angel and turned to look where he was pointing. The moment she saw me, she dropped the basket with the linen to the ground.

'Aiiiii, Mary, Mother of God!' she yelled, as the blood drained from her face. 'Help! Help me, neighbours! Heeeeelp! I'm going to faint! I'm going to die . . . A black cat!'

A window opened with force. Then another one. Scores of open windows were filled with alarmed faces that were looking at me, some with hatred, some with fear, some with hostility and some with disgust! An old lady made the sign of the cross with trembling hands.

'Charge!' came the battle cry from a man in pale green paisley pyjamas, who was hosing down the pavement in front of his house.

'Get it!' echoed the voice of a barber, who dashed out of his nearby shop with a razor in his hands. He was followed by a half-shaven customer with lather on his cheeks and a pocket-knife in his hands. Two old men who were playing backgammon at the corner café started to run after me, brandishing their walking sticks menacingly and shouting threats.

I zoomed through the narrow streets and alleys, missing lampposts by a hair's breadth, crashing into prams, weaving through the legs of housewives laden with vegetables on their way home from the open-air market, while the neighbours from their windows, balconies, terraces, yards and verandas threw at me shoes, clogs, flip-flops, mules, boots, slippers, army boots and pumps – a real shoe-storm, it was. If I had

had the time to collect everything that had been hurled at me I would have been able to open a shoe store, no doubt.

I went round a couple of corners, jumped into a yard with peppermint and basil growing in tin pots, climbed on to a roof and, through a door that had been left ajar, I slipped into a laundry room. I took a quick look around. To my good luck, underneath a window with cracked glass panes at the far end of the room, my eye caught sight of a wooden washing tub. I wriggled under the tub, which smelled of green soap, and held my breath. Then I saw them. Those blue eyes. I saw them gleam like dark gems in the dim light. Apparently, there was another cat hiding in the same place. And yet, those tender eyes looked familiar. I was sure I knew that cat from somewhere! When I finally saw the rose-coloured velvet ribbon with the silver bell tied round her neck, I was certain.

'Ebonina!' I mewed.

She recognised me. 'Are you in hiding, too?' she asked.

'Unfortunately, or, now that I met you, I should say fortunately.'

'Are they after you?'

'Like hell.'

'Who would have thought that we'd meet as fugitives in a laundry room, under a washing tub.'

We started talking. I had this urgent need to talk to someone, to open up my heart. We talked about a thousand things, about this and about that. I learned that Graziella and

Rasmin had become a couple. On the day of the mating ceremony they had served the guests croquettes of shrimp and the couple had been showered with dozens of expensive gifts.

'Do you know what Mrs Camilla Caprizioni gave them?' she asked me.

'What?'

'A ball of golden wool so that they can play together.'

'Do you still love him?' I asked.

'Who?'

'You know who. Rasmin.'

'Oh, no.' She answered without the slightest hesitation. 'He was vain, capricious and fussy. He watched me as I stood waiting outside the window day after day and didn't deign to speak to me even once. If the maid was just five minutes late with his breakfast, he deliberately peed on his cushion just to make her clean it for him.'

'Are you in love with another cat, now?'

'No, I'm not.'

I hesitated for a while but then I came right out with it. 'Would you be able to love a cat like me?'

'Of course I would!'

I could feel her warmth. I tried to guess at the velvet secrets buried in her eyes. I could hear the distant, happy voices of a group of girls playing hopscotch in the street. A ray of sun fell on to a pool of soapy water and the seven colours of the rainbow flashed fleetingly. I nibbled gently at her ear. She bit mine back. She rubbed her muzzle against mine. I felt a sweet shiver down my spine. We curled up together under the tub, and purred one another to sleep.

When we woke up a soft, light rain had started. The raindrops rapped rhythmically on to the dusty windows of the laundry room.

'Ebonina!' I mewed.

She looked at me tenderly. And, as if by a miracle, now everything seemed less hopeless, less threatening than before. I had someone to love me now, to care for me and share my hopes and fears. We were together now. Together, we could face any danger, together we would mange to pull through, together we would find a way to survive.

And, as if to confirm my thoughts, the door to the laundry room half opened and the world seemed brighter all around, as the dimpled face of a young girl appeared at the opening. She saw us, but she wasn't scared, she didn't start yelling, she didn't go after us. She just smiled, closed the door conspiratorially and came near us. She bent down, whispering tenderly, she touched us softly, she caressed our ears. Before she left, she took a few soft-roasted chick-peas out of her pocket and offered them to us. I can't say that chick-peas are my favourite food, nor Ebonina's, but we were so hungry that we ate them gratefully before you could say 'fish pie in the sky'.

From then on, our protecting angel would secretly bring

us food and water, whenever she had the chance. Sometimes it was a pot of yoghurt, sometimes a meatball, sometimes a single strand of spaghetti tied in a knot, sometimes whitebait tails and then sometimes delectable anchovy heads.

Every Friday, when her mother came up to the laundry room to do the week's washing, the girl smuggled us into her room, and let us hide in the box with the wind-up crocodile, the fancy coloured top and the rest of her toys. We learned that her name was Marilena and that she used to have a black kitten, which had been taken from her when the great persecution started, despite her protests. Her face flooded with tears, she begged them in vain to let her keep it. That's why she had felt such joy when she had so unexpectedly found us in the laundry room. Only on the morning she brought us a ball made out of tin foil to play with, did it cross my mind that our new friend could be Marilena, the girl Tarmac had talked about that night on the bridge.

And so the days rolled by until one day, as we were chasing after a butterfly outside the washing room, one of the neighbours, a middle-aged lady in a faded dressing gown, who was drying plum tomatoes in the sun on the terrace next door, saw us. She said nothing, but there was a nasty, devious glint in her eyes. She stood there for a couple of minutes with her hands on her hips, shaking her head in disapproval. Then she went on with her work and, when she had finished, she disappeared downstairs.

'Do you think she'll turn us in?' Ebonina asked.

'I'm not sure, but I'd say we'd better leg it anyway!'

'No, Let's not go yet! It's so nice here. Marilena loves us so much – she takes such good care of us.'

'But Ebonina, we are in danger. If the neighbour squeals on us, what will happen then?'

'Why should she do that? Besides, well ... didn't you notice?'

'Notice what?'

'She was way too old. She probably couldn't see very well. She might have mistaken us for swallows.'

'All right,' I relented. 'Let's wait and see.'

We curled up together in the washing tub. A thousand soap bubbles danced around us. We had almost fallen asleep when we heard the wail of the sirens from the approaching police cars.

21

The ferret by the brook

In which an old horse recalls past glories and a shifty-looking ferret talks to Ebonina by the brook.

A nd so we were forced to leave the hospitable laundry room, without even saying goodbye to Marilena. For hours on end, we wandered from place to place, before we finally found shelter under an upturned boat down at the harbour.

As the days went by, things progressed from bad to worse. One cat betrayed another. You hardly knew who was your friend and who was your enemy, any more. Several con-cats snatched the opportunity and arranged to smuggle or hide cats for a fee and then denounced them to get the reward money on top of their extortionate fees.

Deceit, betrayal and knavery abounded. Various self-proclaimed inventors, Federico Firenze among them, sold black cats their apocryphal recipes for whitening. A cunning crook even claimed that he had found a way to make black cats invisible. But the worst of all was the swans.

One day, in the park, I heard loud voices and commotion. I climbed up an oak tree and saw yet another dead swan being pulled out of the water of the lake. His long, lifeless neck hung limply from the arms of the keeper who was carrying him.

'What's going on? What's happened to the swan?' I asked a squirrel with a bushy tail who was crunching a hazelnut on the next branch.

'It appears that one of your lot attacked it!' the squirrel replied, with a reproachful look.

'Why?'

'Come on now. As if you don't know . . .'

'Know what?'

'There's a rumour about.'

'What rumour is that?'

'That if a black cat wants to turn white, it has to taste the heart of a swan.'

I was thunderstruck. 'Does this thing happen often?' I asked.

'What thing?'

I nodded in the direction of the dead swan in the keeper's arms.

'Every now and then. They usually drown themselves but they sometimes kill the swans first.'

'Have you ever seen this? Have you seen a black cat kill

a swan with your own eyes?' I insisted.

'No, but I've heard people talk about it.'

Before I had time to ask any more questions, the squirrel jumped on to the neighbouring oak tree.

Now I knew what Cottontail's and the other cats' mutterings and innuendos meant. What have we come to? I thought. What has mankind's persecution led us to?

On the days that followed, the incidents with the dead swans increased. The attacks fed mass hysteria and people viewed these cruel killings as confirmation of their superstitions and proof that black cats were indeed dangerous beasts. There were those, on the other hand, who maintained that the Guardians of Good Luck killed the swans on purpose and blamed cats in order to turn even reasonable people against them.

Besides this, the majority of the population had been overcome with a more general aversion to all things dark. They wanted to whiten everything. Everything had to be whiter than white. They were thrown into a whitening frenzy. They whitewashed their houses furiously. Wholesale merchants who dealt in white sugar, white rice and white bread were making a fortune. Even at funeral processions the undertakers were not dressed in black any more. They wore cream-coloured suits, lime green bow ties, yellow braces and pink shoelaces.

My darling Ebonina and I lived in constant fear for our

lives. We changed our hiding place at regular intervals to make it harder for people to track us down. In turn, we hid inside a circus cannon, underneath a laundry basket, in an old train wagon, on the roof of a pizza restaurant, even in the darkroom of a photographer who specialised in wedding photos. Every time the photographer came into his darkroom to develop photos of the newlyweds, we shut our eyes tight so that they wouldn't shine in the dark and betray our presence. At nights, when he fell asleep, we ventured out of the darkroom and stole whatever we could lay our paws on from the cellar or the kitchen.

When, one day, the photographer finally detected our presence, we had to run away again, before he drowned us in the basin with the developing fluid, as he threatened to do while chasing after us.

We wandered for two or three days and nights until, to our good fortune, we chanced upon a farmyard and found refuge in a manger with two old horses that mumbled and grumbled from dusk to dawn because they were pestered by horseflies. One of them had hurt his leg and feared that if it didn't get any better soon, they might decide to put him down. Sometimes he yearned for the time when he was free to gallop in the meadows and could rear up on his strong hind legs and neigh at the top of his lungs, proud, powerful and untamed. The other horse rarely spoke.

'What kind of animals are you?' the old horse with the

wounded leg asked me one day. His eyes were infected, too, and he couldn't see very well.

'Cats.'

'Black cats?'

'Yes.'

'The kind they say brings bad luck . . .'

'Yes, that kind! But what they say is not true.'

'I know.'

'How do you know?'

'People will say anything. Don't listen to them. They claim, fools that they are, that horseshoes bring good luck. If you take myself for example, my dear bats.'

'Sorry, we're cats.'

'If you take myself for example, my dear cats, I wear not one but four horseshoes and see what good they did to me. Look! I've got a crippled leg, bad eyesight and an uncertain future. Horseshoes are lucky! Ha! Allow me to neigh!'

Another day, the old horse started to tell me the story of his life. He said that before he got old and was sold to the farm, he served in the cavalry of a select battalion and took part in glorious parades, walking proud, beautifully dressed and decorated. He remembered with particular emotion one spring day when the army band played a march and the officers' medals sparkled in the sunlight, as the people crowding the streets cheered and applauded . . .

While the horse, deeply moved by his own memories,

talked, his eyes filled with tears, I saw Ebonina through the half-open door of the barn. She was by the gurgling brook that ran through the farm, speaking to a ferret in hushed tones.

I asked the old horse to excuse me and ran to see what was going on. Before I got anywhere near them, though, the ferret legged it as fast as it could.

'Who was that?' I asked, curiously, a strange feeling gripping my heart.

'Oh, just a ferret that was passing by.'

'What was he saying to you?'

'Nothing,' replied Ebonina, with a guilty look in her eyes.

'But he was saying something to you!' I insisted.

'He was telling me about his . . .' She hesitated. '. . . about his grandmother.'

'What was he saying about her?'

'Well . . . that she's sick and he's trying to get her some healing herbs. He was asking if we've got any snake-root or mountain mint on the farm.'

Something inside me told me that she was lying, but I never had the chance to confront her, as from behind the ferns that grew next to the brook, there appeared a black muzzle. And not just any muzzle. I most definitely knew that muzzle. It was Tarmac's.

I hadn't seen him for a long time and I was over the

moon. 'Hey, Tarmac, you old fraud!'

He jumped for joy at seeing me once again. So did I. He had happened to hit on this farm as he was trying to escape from some boys who were throwing stones at him. I introduced him to Ebonina. The news he brought was very bad. He informed us that besides ourselves, all other black cats had been exterminated. I felt a cold, steely hand gripping my heart.

'How can you be sure?' I asked.

'I heard a newspaper-seller cry out that there are only three black cats left on the island and whoever finds them will receive the decoration of the Order of the Four-Leafed Clover from the Minister of Public Order himself.'

'You know what?' I said, to change the subject and cheer him up. 'I've got a surprise for you.'

'What is it?'

'Something that will make you really happy!'

'Come on! Tell!'

'I think we've met your Marilena.'

'That's impossible!'

'Oh, no it isn't . . .'

I described in detail what had happened at the laundry room where I had sought shelter with Ebonina. I told him about the girl with the dimpled cheeks, the whitebait tails, the lengths of spaghetti tied in a knot and the balls made of tin foil that she brought us to play with.

'Yes, it must be her!' Tarmac agreed. 'The house where we lived did not have a laundry room, though. They must have moved.'

We went on talking, but from that moment on, Tarmac seemed preoccupied. He paced restlessly up and down all the time.

'What's got into you? What's wrong?' I asked, although I feared I knew the answer.

'I can't stand it any longer, you guys. It's beyond me. Now that you've reminded me of her, I need to go and find her.'

'It's way too dangerous.' I tried to dissuade him.

'If she could hide you, then she'll hide me, too. You can't imagine how much I long to see her. Believe me!'

'But there's the neighbour – the one who called the police. Think about it. You're in danger . . .'

It was impossible to talk him out of it. He had made up his mind. He was determined to visit Marilena.

'I don't care how dangerous it is. I'm going to see her. How about it? Can I stay with you for the night and set off tomorrow morning?'

'Of course you can.'

The sun had already started to set. The shadows were getting longer. Night would soon fall. We were about to head for the barn, when we heard a gunshot.

All three of us swiftly hid behind some thick bushes with small purple flowers.

'Do you think they've found us?' Tarmac whispered, terrified.

'No, I think I know what that was about.'

I was right. When it was dark enough for us to return safely to the barn, one of the two old horses was gone. The four lucky horseshoes he was wearing were not enough protection from the cruelty of people.

22

The grannies in the playground

In which Tarmac is reunited with Marilena at the playground but his joy is short-lived.

The following morning, Tarmac woke up at the crack of dawn and couldn't wait to set off. I went along to show him where Marilena lived now. Ebonina wanted to join us, too, but I managed to persuade her to stay behind and wait for us at the farm. As things turned out it was a blessing she did not insist and was spared from witnessing what happened next.

We went to the town, following secluded paths, narrow roads and shady cobbled streets.

When, after a long time and many detours, we finally managed to reach Marilena's house, we saw her go out the front door, holding the hand of an elderly lady who must have been her granny. Marilena was wearing a purple ribbon in her hair and was carrying a little bucket. Her granny had a knitted shawl with long fringes across her shoulders, and a big straw bag hung from her arm.

'What do you think we should do?' I whispered. 'Shall we wait for them to come back?'

'No. Let's follow them.'

So we did. We followed them cautiously to the playground. When we got there we climbed up an elm tree and sneaked a peek from there. There weren't very many people at the playground that day. Two boys with grazed knees were on a see-saw, a little girl with violet eyes and golden hair played with a skipping rope, a couple of kind-looking grannies were sitting on a bench under the shade of an orange tree, knitting. One had hair as white as cotton, and was wearing a pair of small, round glasses. She was knitting a bubblegum-pink baby jacket. The other, whose hands were shaking slightly, was knitting light-blue booties. Purl one, knit one, purl one, knit one, purl one, knit one . . .

Marilena's granny chose a bench beside a flowering shrub and took a piece of embroidery out of her bag. Marilena went on the slide once or twice. Then she took her little bucket, ran to the sand-pit and started to build castles and palaces. Everything was so calm, so peaceful. It was as if people's malice could not touch this tranquil place . . .

'I'll go and talk to her. I can't wait any longer,' whispered Tarmac.

'No! Not yet,' I advised him. 'Hold on! Let's wait until she goes back home and then we'll see. It's far too public, here.'

'I want to be with her now.'

'Get a grip!'

'I'm going!'

Before I could stop him, he jumped off our leafy hiding place and ran towards the girl. Marilena saw him. She jumped up. Her face lit up. She let out a cry of joy. She was about to start running towards him eagerly. But she never made it. A sharp stone whizzed in the air. It got him just behind the ear. Tarmac lost his balance. He crumpled into the sand-pit.

The granny who had thrown the stone sat back on the bench, picked up the bootie that she had put by her side and went on knitting. Knit one, purl one, knit one, purl one, knit one, purl one, knit one, purl one . . . She just sat there knitting, as if nothing had happened.

Tarmac was writhing in the sand-pit. I could hear his hoarse breathing. Then, the second granny got up, pulled the knitting needle out of the baby jacket, went near Tarmac and pushed it right through his heart. Then, calm and collected, she returned to her seat, wiped the bloody needle with a lacy handkerchief and continued knitting with a blank look on her face. Knit one, purl one, knit one, purl one, knit one, purl one, knit one, purl one . . .

The red stain was slowly seeping into the sand round Tarmac. His eyes looked at the girl one more time, full of longing. Then they closed. Marilena stood there, motionless, unable to grasp what had just happened. She shook violently. Suddenly, she started to scream. She screamed again and again, burying her face in her hands. They were such shrill, desperate screams that they pierced your ears and made your heart bleed.

'Please don't do that, my precious angel,' her granny said soothingly and took her by the hand. 'That darned cat would have brought you bad luck. It was a blessing that the ladies acted in time to avert the evil. Come now, let's go!'

Marilena followed obediently, muffling her sobs.

Then, one by one, everyone left without a word. The boys with the grazed knees, the little girl, the two grannies . . .

Tarmac lay there, in the bloodstained pit, next to the crumpled sandcastle, a sorrowful sight in the middle of the playground.

I heard a bee buzz, a tap drip slowly and a junk dealer's voice cry in the distance, 'I'll buy your old clothes and china. I'll buy all your junk!'

Then I left, too.

23

The last couple

*In which our hero tries to give his sweetheart courage,
but she has something else in mind.*

Ebonina was waiting impatiently back at the farm.
'What happened? Did he find Marilena?' she asked me
when I arrived.

'He did but –'

'But what?'

I told her what had happened in all detail. She remained
silent for quite a long time.

'It's just the two of us, then!' she finally said.

'So it seems. But don't despair, my purrcious!' I consoled
her, trying to pluck some courage from my own words. 'All is
not lost. There's still –'

'Still what?'

'There's still hope.'

'You don't really believe that!'

'Oh, but I *do* believe it! They might have wiped out

all other black cats, but – but –'

'But what?'

'There's still the two of us. We . . .'

'We?' Ebonina laughed bitterly. 'What can *we* do? What can we possibly *do*?'

'Kittens. Black kittens! And they will have other kittens, in turn . . . Black cats won't be lost for ever.'

She didn't speak. Just looked at me with sorrowful eyes. 'Why don't we change colour?' she asked quietly. Her voice was barely audible.

'What are you talking about, Ebonina? Besides, that's impossible.'

'I've heard that there are ways in which one could change colour and become white.'

'Please don't listen to all this. It's either a hoax or an illusion. One of the two.'

'I love you.'

'I know.'

'I want us to live – to survive. What does colour matter? What does it matter if we aren't black, any more?'

'But I've told you. It can't be done.'

'How can you be so sure?'

'Listen to me when I'm talking. I used to know someone who tried and failed. His name was Federico Firenze. Don't ask . . . Don't torment me!'

'All right,' Ebonina whispered. 'Snuggle up close to me.

I'm cold, so very cold.'

I moved close to her. We both curled up, side by side and looked through the window over the manger at the moon being chased by the clouds in the sky. She fell asleep. I didn't. I went on looking at the clouds that kept changing colour and shape all the time. I saw them become castles and palaces and fantastic beasts – unicorns, dragons and griffins – and then exotic galleons that floated on waves of jasmine blossom.

If I were a ship's cat . . . If only I had left . . . If I had travelled somewhere far away . . . If . . .

24

The magpie and her gang

In which our hero follows his loved one into a wood with chestnut trees and sees her meet a magpie and her suspicious-looking friends.

'I must go somewhere, but I don't want you to come with me!' Ebonina said a few days later.

'Why?'

'I'm preparing a surprise for you.'

'What kind of surprise?'

'It won't be a surprise if I tell you.'

'Tell the me the first letter, at least.'

'Don't be a naughty boy. I won't say anything for now. Bear in mind that I might be a little late, though, but don't worry – I will certainly be back before it gets dark.'

'There's no way I'll let you go alone.'

'Why?'

'Do you need to ask why? These are difficult times, my darling Ebonina. There's danger behind every step, there's a trap lying round every corner!'

'I'll be careful. I promise I will.'

'But why do you insist on going alone?'

'I've already told you. It's a surprise. Promise you won't follow me?'

'Oh, all right!' I was forced to promise. 'You be careful, though. Keep your eyes peeled!'

The minute I saw her leave, I changed my mind. I had a premonition that something would go wrong, something bad would happen. On the other hand, I wasn't a hundred per cent sure. I decided to follow her from a discreet distance and see where she was going.

It was a sunny afternoon with a light breeze and bumble-bees buzzing in the bushes all around me. I followed Ebonina as she crossed the stream with the purple reeds, the valley with the wild cyclamen and the spinney with the leafy elm tees and reached the wood with the lovesick woodpeckers.

'Hi! Where are you off to?' I heard a familiar tweet.

It was Wallace the woodpecker. He was perched on one of the branches of the walnut tree with the twelve hearts and was looking at me. His broken wing had mended and looked as good as new.

I signalled to him not to betray my presence. He understood and kept quiet. I walked on, trying not to lose sight of Ebonina even for one moment. I shuddered at the thought that anything bad might happen to her. I moved silently among the blackberry bushes and the wild flowers with my ears pricked, ready to step in at once if I saw any threat to her.

Ebonina left the wood with the lovesick woodpeckers behind her, skirted the meadow with the beehives, crossed a stone bridge and arrived at the wood with the red chestnut trees, where a weasel with tiny, crafty eyes was waiting for her.

'Hello, Lily!' Ebonina greeted her cheerfully.

'Hello, there, Ebonina! You look very pretty today!' the weasel greeted her in a voice as sweet as sticky honey. 'Welcome! Let me introduce my colleagues. This is Isabella the magpie and Knups the ferret.'

An old magpie jumped on to a low branch and a ferret with a shifty look emerged from the hollow of a chestnut tree. I recognised it immediately. It was the same ferret that had been talking to her by the brook a few days ago.

'You've already met Knups, I believe.'

'Indeed I have. He's the one who first told me about you and your valuable services.'

'Well? Have you made a decision? Are you ready for the change?'

'Yes ... but ... I'm not sure what I'm doing is right.' Ebonina hesitated.

'No, no, no, I won't have this! What are you saying, sweetheart? Of course it's right! And proper!'

'Nowadays it's terribly dangerous, it's practically suicide

for anyone to be of a black colour,' seconded the magpie.

'But are you sure I'll change colour? Will I definitely become white?'

'But of course, my lovely!' Lily the weasel assured her.

'Pure white!' Knups the ferret jumped in.

'As white as icing sugar! Whiter than snow!' crowed Isabella the magpie.

'Please, have complete faith in us,' Lily said. 'We are professionals. We know what we're doing. We've got loads of experience in these matters. But let us not waste time. We'll start as soon as we collect our payment.'

'You want me to pay right now?'

'Well, yes, if you don't mind . . . So that we don't hold you up later,' said Knups, with an avaricious glint in his shifty eyes.

'All right! Take it then!' Ebonina conceded.

I saw Knups the ferret and Lily the weasel undo the rose-coloured velvet ribbon with the tiny silver bell, remove it from Ebonina's neck, and give it to Isabella the magpie, who held it up carefully, examined it with an expert eye, pecked at it with her beak and hung it on a twig, together with about a dozen ribbons of all colours: blue, mauve, orange, pink, yellow, violet, some with gold and others with little silver bells that sparkled splendidly in the setting sun.

'Did they all belong to cats that have changed colour?' asked Ebonina.

'But of course! They belonged to cats who now lead a blissful life, with no one being any the wiser of their dark past!' explained Lily. 'Come now, my pretty one. Follow me.'

'Where are we going?'

'Where else? To the magical Lake of White Hope. Every night, the brightest stars of the galaxy fall into its still waters like a dreamy, sparkling rain.'

Ebonina made her farewells to Isabella the magpie and Knups the ferret, who pretended to sniff back their tears because of their sorrow to see her go, and followed Fiona the weasel.

I followed them stealthily. I was determined to get to the bottom of this and reveal the machinations of those impostors – for this is what they were, all three of them, no doubt. I don't deny that I was rather curious to see that strange lake. The Lake of White Hope. The lake in whose still waters the brightest stars of the galaxy fell every night like a dreamy, sparkling rain.

I trod lightly on the sodden, rotting leaves. I tried not to make any noise, lest they detected my presence, but I had the unpleasant feeling that I too was being followed. I wasn't sure, though. I turned round sharply once or twice and looked behind me, but I saw no one.

Lily the weasel and Ebonina walked across the wood with the red chestnut trees, which was getting darker by the minute as night began to fall.

'Are we still far from the Lake of White Hope?' asked Ebonina some time later.

'We'll be there any minute now, sweetie pie ... Be patient!' I heard Lily say.

They came out on the other side of the wood with the towering trees. They went through a vineyard, over a bridge beside a water mill and soon they arrived at a quarry. And there I saw it. I finally saw the Lake of White Hope gleaming dreamily in the moonlight. I hadn't expected that. It really was white – pure white; it was out of this world.

Could it be? I thought, spellbound.

'Here we are!' announced Lily the weasel.

'Is this the Lake of White Hope?' asked Ebonina, her breath taken away with surprise, joy and unbearable expectation.

'That's exactly what it is, sweetie pie. See, I wasn't lying!'

'What should I do now?'

'What else? Pick up speed and jump right in.'

'Is that what I should do?'

'Naturally! If you jump in, if you swim across this white dream, you'll come out the other side as white as the purest snow.'

'That's wonderful!'

'Only – you should think of changing your name after that. Ebonina won't suit you any more. I'd suggest another name like, Bianca, White Pearl or Albinina. What do you say?'

'I'll think about it . . . May I ask you something?'

'Yes, dear.'

'Could I bring my fiancé so that he becomes white, too?'

'But of course. Why not?'

'Well, you see, he's a stray cat. He hasn't got a ribbon or a silver bell to pay you with.'

'Never mind. In his case, we'll make an exception. You can bring him any time you like!'

'Free of charge?'

'Naturally, seeing that you love him so much. Love is a wonderful thing.'

'You are so good to me.'

'Indeed, goodness of heart is one of my many virtues.'

'Are there more?'

'More what?'

'Virtues.'

'Oh, countless. Lots and lots, my little one – but we'll be standing here all night if I start counting them. Are you ready?'

'Yes, I am.'

'Off you go then, and when you get to the shore, take a deep breath and jump! Jump right into the lake! Forget everything! Leave the past behind you! Let yourself sink deep into the dreams of faraway galaxies. Farewell, my pretty one! Farewell!'

I saw Ebonina bid Lily goodbye and walk slowly towards the White Lake. It was truly white, this lake. There was no doubt about it. Something nagged at me, though. There was something about the glistening surface that was not quite right. My intuition told me that the three crooks had set up some terrible fraud, too terrible to imagine.

It had gone too far. I had to step in. I had to reveal myself and warn Ebonina, who had almost reached the shores of the White Lake. I was going to stop her – although she would be disappointed, she would blame me, she would be mad at me for breaking my promise not to follow her!

'Ebonina!' I was about to cry. But I didn't make it. The meow died in my throat as I received a strong blow on the head and fell unconscious. Before I lost my senses, I just had time to see Knups, the ferret, lean over my body, sniggering, with a block of wood in his paws. After that, I plunged into darkness.

25

The Lake of White Hope

In which our hero learns the bitter truth about the heavenly Lake of White Hope.

When I came to, all was quiet and desolate around me. Knups the ferret, Lily the weasel and – worst of all – my beloved Ebonina weren't anywhere to be seen. Only the Lake of White Hope continued to glimmer, a heavenly vision in the pale moonlight.

'Ebonina!' I cried.

There was no answer. Only deadly silence around me.

'Ebonina!' I cried again, as a horrible premonition rose inside me, like a violent wave. 'Ebonina! My purrcious Ebonina!'

'What happened? Why are you howling like that?' came a hoarse, angry voice.

A tortoise with a dark-green shell and heavy, wrinkled folds on her head and legs, was shuffling awkwardly towards me.

'Where's Ebonina?' I asked.

'Ebonina? What is this Ebonina? Is it a tortoise?'

'No. She's a cat. A black cat. Pitch black.'

'Oh, is she one of those poor souls Lily the weasel lures down here?'

I did not like the word 'lures' one little bit. It confirmed my worst suspicions. 'Yes . . . What happened to her? Did she swim across the Lake of White Hope? Did she manage to get to the other side? Did she change colour? Did she become white?'

The tortoise shook her wrinkly head with pity, but said nothing.

'Speak!' I yelled. 'Speak, old tortoise! What happened? Tell me! Did she jump? Did she become white? Why are you looking at me like that?'

'Move on, young lad,' the old tortoise replied. 'It's best if you never learn the truth. Go on your way and forget all about Ebonina . . .' And with these words, she retreated into her dark-green shell.

'Please come out again,' I implored her. 'Please come out for half a minute. Please come out, old tortoise.'

It seemed that she felt sorry for me because I saw her head emerge from her shell again.

'What happened? Tell me! Why aren't you talking to me?'

'The truth is bitter, youngster.'

'I don't care how bitter it is, I need to know!'

'It will hurt you very much, if I tell you.'

'Tell me . . . I'm begging you. Speak, tortoise. Speak!'

And then the old tortoise spoke. Her deep, hollow voice seemed to be coming from the depths of time. She said, 'Lily the weasel is a liar. She's a treacherous thief and her wrongdoings have no end. Her words are a delusion. Her evil defies description. The same goes for Isabella the magpie and Knups the ferret! The whole damned gang!'

So, my suspicions were right. 'What about the Lake of White Hope? I've never seen such a lake before. Such dream-like beauty. Such magical splendour . . .'

'The Lake of White Hope is the Lake of Black Doom.'

'What do you mean?'

'You don't want to know.'

'Tell me!'

'The Lake of White Hope, my lad, is just a –'

'What?'

The tortoise hesitated. I looked at her. It was as if her wrinkles had sunk even deeper. Forgotten prophecies were reflected fleetingly in her misty eye. 'A pool of quicklime,' she said, in a voice that was barely audible.

I couldn't believe my ears. 'Do you mean . . .?'

'Yes. Once Lily has robbed her victims of their little treasures, she leads them here, to their certain and most horrid death. The cats that have believed her jump in of their own free will, hoping to find happiness in the Lake of White Hope. In reality, they plunge into a white tomb of excruciating pain. This leaves no witnesses and her gang can continue to commit their foul crimes undisturbed.'

I just stood there motionless, silent, trying to grasp the enormity of what the old tortoise had said to me. 'Did you see her jump with your own eyes?' I asked.

The tortoise nodded her wrinkled head. 'When an evil thing starts, it spreads like wildfire!' she said. 'That's true, my lad. One bad thing brings a million others. Everyone capitalises on the persecution. My eyes have seen a lot. Truly a lot.'

So the old tortoise spoke, and then she fell silent, looked at me pityingly one more time and walked away slowly.

I was left alone. Never in my life had I felt so alone. Slowly, I moved close to the edge of that deceitful lake. I climbed on to a pile of discarded wood planks nearby. There was not a trace of Ebonina. Only the white, smooth surface.

'Ebonina . . .' I muttered to myself.

I loved her. I loved her so much. I loved her smooth, shiny coat, her blue, velvety eyes. I loved her but she was no more. I had lost her for ever . . . I tried to picture her agony, her despair as the burning quicklime sucked her in greedily and dragged her down.

Suddenly, the planks slipped from under my feet and rolled down, one after the other. I lost my footing and barely managed to jump to the side before I was myself thrown into the deceptive pool.

At the same time I heard barking. There were wolfhounds! Torches shone all around me. Cries and the thud of heavy footsteps were heard in the darkness. The weasel and her accomplice must have denounced me.

And then, for the first time, I realised the extent of the disaster. All the other black cats had been exterminated. Even my beloved Ebonina. I was alone. Completely alone in a nightmarish, ruthless world. Without a friend, without a companion, without the slightest hope. My time had come. Inevitable and inexorable, my end was near, too. I didn't have the will or the strength to fight any more. Even the last shred of courage had left me. I had to admit it – our persecutors had achieved their goal.

But no, they hadn't quite achieved their goal – yet. If they aimed at eliminating all black cats, as long as one, just a single one of us lived, they hadn't yet succeeded. And *I* was alive. That was precisely the reason why I had to get out of it. I had to save myself in any way possible, by any means, no matter what the cost! I had to survive and avenge Ebonina's, Purrcy's and Tarmac's unjust deaths along with every other black cat's. If I didn't do it then who would? Who would be left to remember them?

There, over Ebonina's silent, white grave, under the dark, starless sky, I swore that I wouldn't let our persecutors triumph! I would do anything in my power to evade them! I knew that they would hound me pitilessly with any devious means, any deceptive trappings, any infernal ruse they could think of.

I'd show them, indeed! I'd fly in the face of their hatred. I'd fight their madness. They wouldn't catch me. I wouldn't let them annihilate me! No! Not me!

All around me, the murderous cries of the mob were getting louder. The flaming torches had almost surrounded me . . . The furious barking of the wolfhounds kept drawing closer . . .

The platter of bonito

In which a delicious platter of bonito turns into a deadly trap.

The sweet smell of sardines. The sublime, irresistible aroma of delicious sardines. If there's something I am totally overpowered by, it is the smell of sardines. It literally drives me crazy. Sheer delight . . .

I traced the smell down to a fish market. It was deserted. Not a soul in sight. No cat, no fisherman, not one fishmonger, not a single customer. To the left and to the right, crates packed full of sardines formed a glorious avenue that led up to a table laid with white linen and a platter full of fresh, firm bonito. And if there's something I love more than sardines, it is mouthwatering bonito.

As if in a trance, I started to walk towards the fish platter. I must have been about ten metres away from it, when the white tablecloth was lifted and the barrel of a flame-thrower appeared from under it.

With a swift move I managed to miss the jet of white flame that darted at me. At the same time, the barrels of guns appeared from between the crates of sardines all around me. Dozens of barrels spat fire. As if I were in a shooting range, I started to zig-zag to save myself. One bullet scraped by my tail. Another nicked my ear.

I woke up with a start. What a nightmare! I found myself lying in the hollow of the red chestnut tree, where I'd hidden the night before to escape my persecutors and their hounds. Luckily, I had managed to get back to the forest by following my route to the lake in reverse. The whole of my body ached. I got out of the hollow and jumped into the grass. The rays of the sun slipped through the branches of the trees. Their green foliage glimmered softly in the rosy hues of the early sunlight. Behind a cluster of trees, a deer peeked at me fleetingly and off it went like a blue streak. I lapped up some water from a gurgling brook and licked my dusty fur clean. I looked for the gang of the magpie but found no one. There was no sign of Isabella, Lily or Knups.

From that day on, wherever I went I was hunted down. My whole life became a ceaseless persecution. A chase without mercy, without end. If people weren't shooting at me, they threw daggers, and if they weren't throwing daggers, they emptied pans of scalding water over me. I had to hide all the time, I had to lie low, duck and weave, slide like a shadow. I had to make myself completely inconspicuous.

I changed my hiding place every now and then. For about a month, I lived on the back seat of an old, battered jeep that had broken down, in a car graveyard. Then I sought refuge in a dark tunnel. It was highly unlikely that they would have gone looking for me in there, but my blood curdled every time the express train hurtled past only inches from my whiskers.

In the end I could take no more and I changed residence yet again. I discovered an abandoned wooden pigeon-loft among the ruins of a derelict farmhouse, near the brook with the reeds and slept there during the day. It was safer to look for food when it was dark. I lived on cicadas, crickets, spiders, lizards, even centipedes. Sometimes, if I was lucky, I caught a fish in the shallow waters of the brook, but that didn't happen very often. There were other times when, blinded by hunger, I went to the town, flying in the face of danger, and did the rubbish-bin rounds.

27

The fishbone tree

In which our hero finds the tree of his dreams, which, however, turns into a nightmare, while three fowls find his troubles amusing.

One night, as I was walking along the pavement, hungry, almost famished, I found myself in front of a tree that was completely different from any other. I confess, I'd never seen such a tree before, or, to be precise, I'd seen one like it only in my dreams.

Fishbones hung from its branches. Delicious, scrumptious, luscious, mouthwatering fishbones. I had obviously had the incredible luck to come across a perennial fishbone tree. In the old times, when I was planning to become a ship's cat and sail around the world, I used to imagine that one day I might find myself shipwrecked on a desert island, thick with precisely this type of tree, and live there blissfully ever after.

I blinked a couple of times, just in case what I was seeing

was a mirage – a figment of my imagination triggered by weeks of starvation. It wasn't a mirage. It wasn't a figment of my imagination or a hungry vision. It was most certainly a tropical, rare and hard to find – maybe even the only – fishbone tree in the world! Its trunk shimmered in the moonlight. On its branches, dozens of fishbones swayed lightly in the night breeze, as if they were waiting for me to sample them.

I had a good look round. There was not a soul in sight. I walked about the area, but saw nothing suspicious. It was dead silent. The doors were closed. The windows of the houses were shut. I made up my mind! I'd go up the tree! I'd throw myself at the fishbones and stuff my face until I burst! I dug my claws into the trunk of the divine tree and started to climb. Almost immediately I felt something slimy wetting my belly and my paws. These tropical fishbone trees had very strange trunks, I thought. But the higher I climbed, the harder I found it to move, until I realised that it was impossible to go on any further. Not only couldn't I climb any higher, but I couldn't move, either. That slimy thing I'd felt on my belly and paws had hardened now and kept me stuck hard and fast to the tree trunk.

It must be a trap, I thought. I'd walked, or rather climbed, right into it. Some shrewd human had hung fishbones on the branches of the tree and had smeared its trunk with glue! I had come to a sticky end, as if I were a rookie!

There was no doubt about it. I was stuck for good – a prisoner of the treacherous tree. I could neither move forward nor backward. Not left or right. I could only swish my tail, but what good would that do me?

I was in a right royal fix. Glued to the tree, unable to move, I was at the mercy of my persecutors. I expected them to arrive any minute now and finish me off.

'*Cluck*! *Cluck*! *Cluck*!' I heard someone cackle.

It came from a fat red hen that was approaching from the opposite direction. She stood and looked at me as if I were a highly amusing sight. 'What's happened to you, kit?' she asked.

'I'm stuck, don't you see?'

The hen started cackling again. '*Cluck, cluck, cluck! Cluck, cluck, cluck*! You look funny the way you're stuck up there,' she said. 'Did you know that? *Cluck, cluck, cluck! Cluck, cluck, cluck*! Oh, for the life of me!'

I was going to give her a good piece of my mind, but I needed her. I restrained myself and decided to react with exemplary diplomacy.

'You kind and clever little hen,' I flattered her. 'I'm sure a smart fowl like you can help me get unstuck. Please do something!'

Never in my wildest dreams had I imagined that I would have to beg for a hen's help.

'You're in the soup, mate, aren't you?' I heard her say.

'As you can clearly see, yes, I am. Please, do me a favour. Go and call for some help, you beautiful, tender-hearted and charitable fowl!'

The hen looked at me one more time. Then, without a word, she turned round and left.

Good. She must be going to get some help! I thought to myself, trying to keep my chin up and hold back despair.

I waited in the deserted street, stuck tight to the tree, as if I were madly in love with it. A quarter of an hour went by without anything happening at all.

I had begun to worry, when the red hen showed up again. This time she was accompanied by a plump duck and a snowy goose. Maybe if the three of them pulled me together, I might get unstuck.

'So, you've brought some help, then?' I asked.

'Nope!' said the hen. 'Why should I bring any help?'

'I thought that was what you were going to do,' I complained. 'Wasn't it why you went away?'

'No. You were wrong about that. I went to fetch my friends, Deirdre the duck and Gertrude the goose.'

'Why?'

'I thought they could do with a bit of a laugh, too.' The hen turned to her friends. 'Girls, let me introduce my boyfriend,' she said, and pointed at me. 'I'd say he's rather stuck on me!'

'*Quack, quack, quack, quack, quack*!' Deirdre the duck started to laugh.

'You're a funny girl, Henrietta!' honked Gertrude the goose. 'He's "stuck on you"! *Gonk*! You're hilarious!'

'It's what you might call a "cat collage"!' joked Henrietta.

'*Cluck, cluck, cluck*! . . . *Quack, quack, quack*! . . . *Gonk*!' The three fowls shrieked with laughter.

Deirdre the duck was beside herself and rolled on the pavement, laughing helplessly. 'Goodness, gracious me!' she said. 'I haven't laughed so much in ages!'

They were laughing at my pain. They were having fun with my torment. I was in mortal danger and they were enjoying themselves!

'Get out of my sight, you dimwitted fowls! Get lost you bird-brained featherballs!' I said, having lost my patience.

'Did you hear that, girls? He called us bird-brained featherballs!'

'Oooh! He shouldn't have done that!'

'You bet he shouldn't!'

'I'd say he should receive exemplary punishment!' suggested the hen.

'Oh, yes! Yes!' her friends agreed enthusiastically. 'We must punish him! But how, Henrietta?'

'We should peck at his tail!'

'Good idea!'

'That'll be one for the books! We'll tell everyone we've pecked at a cat's tail!'

They moved closer and, jumping or flapping their wings to reach me, they each pecked once at my tail, giggling like schoolgirls.

'What do you say? Shall we pluck it?' suggested the duck. 'It will look dead funny when it's plucked!'

'If you pluck my tail, there'll be hell to pay!' I tried to ward them off.

'That would be true if you weren't stuck where you are!' The duck shut me up.

'Now we'll pluck it free of charge!' The goose laughed.

They were just about to get on with it, when the red hen stopped short, as if she had remembered something. 'Girls! Girls! We're out of time! Let's go before they find out we've sneaked out of the coop and get into trouble! We'll pluck his tail tomorrow, first thing. It's not as if he's going anywhere!'

'You're right! Let's go!' the other two agreed.

They hurried away, wagging their feathery tails from left to right, exchanging little jokes, cackling and nudging one another.

I was left alone, once again. Time passed. A clock struck midnight in the distance. I made another desperate effort to pull myself away from the tree, but I gave up almost instantly. The slightest move was unbearably painful. I was completely defenceless. I'd be at the mercy of my persecutors should anyone happen to find me.

Glued to the tree as I was, I could see one of the knots of its trunk from such a close distance that it seemed like the relentless eye of fate.

That was when I heard footsteps behind me. They were human footsteps. This was it. They had come to finish me off. I wasn't even able to turn round to face my executioner.

The footsteps drew near. My heart was beating against my teeth. A shadow appeared on the side of the pavement. This was my end.

How are they going to kill me? In which way are they going to bump me off? were my last thoughts as the shadow loomed over me.

28

The night patrol

In which someone helps our hero but two members of
the night patrol step in at the last moment.

'Poor darling, what's happened to you?' I heard a voice. A
kind, familiar voice. It was Mother Reene's.

What a relief that was! What joy! What bliss! What a
blessed stroke of good luck!

'What have those thugs done to you?' she asked tenderly.
'You're really stuck here, poor soul.'

She emptied her tattered bag on to the pavement,
fumbled among the scattered contents, picked up a rusty pair
of nail scissors and carefully, very carefully so as not to hurt
me, started snipping off the hairs that were glued to the tree,
stroking me now and then and encouraging me to be patient.

It was a time-consuming job. When it hurt, and I must
admit that it was unbearably painful at times, I did not
complain. After she had finally managed to free me, she took
me in her arms. I abandoned myself with total trust. She

carefully peeled the dried glue off my paws and claws and stroked my fur. I rubbed my head against her and licked her gnarled hands with gratitude. Then, Mother Reene knelt down, took some leftovers out of a paper bag – half a meatball, a sliver of egg white and the tail of a grilled sardine – and fed me, talking sweetly to me all the while.

I had barely managed to swallow the last morsel when, all of a sudden, a jeep came to a screeching halt at the bend of the street. Its headlights blinded us. Two massively built men from the night patrol, wearing armbands with four-leafed clovers within silver horseshoes, leaped out of it. They had square jaws, spiky hair and cruel eyes. With a desperate wail, I sprang to my feet, climbed up a pole and, from there, jumped on to a window ledge and hid behind two large ceramic pots with flowering marjoram. Every fibre in my body was terribly tense.

The night patrolmen swaggered up to Mother Reene. The first one gave her a hard push that pinned her to the wall. 'Don't you know, you geriatric fool, that it is illegal to feed cats?' he growled.

'We were feeding the last cat, weren't we?' said the second man, his rough hand landing heavily on her face. Mother Reene let out a muffled cry.

'We're arresting you on the charge of catophilia!' barked the first one, kneeing her in the stomach. 'You'll soon be wishing you had never been born, you stinking old hag!'

They grabbed Mother Reene brutally by the shoulders and tried to drag her to the jeep that was waiting at the bend of the road, with its engine running. She resisted with all her strength, although she must have known that she didn't have the slightest hope against them. I watched them push her, kicking her like savage beasts, towards the blinding glare of the headlights. Her hair had come undone, her shawl had been torn, beads of blood trickled from her nose to her wrinkled mouth.

I had to help her. Running the danger of hurting her, I pushed one of the clay pots with all my force and it crashed, bang on to the first officer's head. He fell flat on his back on the pavement. The second man leaned over him, his mouth wide open with surprise. Deciding to stake everything, I sprang into the air, landed on his back and stuck all the nails in my claws into his back as deep as they would go.

Mother Reene seized the opportunity and hobbled off into the darkness. I managed to give him a few more deep scratches before he threw me off his back and on to the pavement slabs, yelling like mad. Blinded with rage and pain, he drew a revolver from his belt and came after me. His partner, wiping the soil off his face, followed, spitting out his broken teeth and swearing heavily. They kept running and shooting at me. Bullets whizzed over my head or hit the ground round my feet. I could hear window shutters open, glass panes break and big chunks of plaster from the walls fall to the ground with a heavy thud as they were hit by bullets.

I took a few turns until I realised they had lost me in the meandering alleys of a poor neighbourhood. I kept on running, though, just to be on the safe side. When I finally stopped, I found myself at the port. While I got my breath back, I had a good look around. Two drunken sailors staggered out of a public house. Several seagulls were picking crumbs at the sea-battered pier, while a gang of dockers were unloading sacks of fragrant coffee from a sailing ship.

I looked carefully around, searching for a hiding place to spend the night. A little further on, I saw a high pile of heavy, rolled-up Persian carpets. I climbed on to the stack and wriggled my way into a gap between the rolls.

29

The secret of the four ships

In which our hero finds out from an old friend what four mysterious ships are hiding in their holds.

'Well, well, well, well! Look who's here! Listen, I've got the most fantastic verse for you!'

I heard a voice. It was Cheapskate, the mouse. That's all I needed now. How had he appeared here, at this time of night? To be honest, I can't say I wasn't happy to see him. Who would have thought that the last friend I'd have left on this earth would turn out to be a mouse? That, after everyone had disowned and abandoned me, a measly mouse would be there for me and offer me comfort in my darkest hour.

'I don't need verses any more!' I cut him short.

'Just listen, will you?' And before I had the chance to stop him, he started to recite:

> *You've got, I'm told, in there*
> *A heart as hard as the gruyere*

What nights of passion we would share
If it was soft as camembert

'Well, what do you think?'

'Good, but useless.'

'Oh, come on, mate! Why such despair?'

I told him everything. Every little detail. I had a great need to talk to someone, to open up my heart.

'You don't say,' he remarked when I had finished. 'Is that so? No wonder you feel so blue. But I am afraid that things are even worse than you imagine! I've got news for you! Earth-shattering news!'

'I know,' I sighed.

'You know nothing! The news I'm about to divulge is as fresh as Uncle Matthew's yoghurt. Why, a friend told me only half an hour ago!'

'Who's that?'

'Orlop, the much-travelled ship's mouse with the tarry tail. Actually, that's why you find me at the port.'

'Oh, yes. I was wondering what you were doing here at this time of the night.'

'Haven't you heard what I said? I was visiting Orlop the sailor mouse. It was his tail's birthday today.'

'What? Does his tail have a separate birthday from the rest of him?'

'Yes, he's very fond of it. Orlop himself celebrates his

birthday once a year but his tail celebrates it twice a month. Today it was its sixty-seventh and a half month birthday, if you please.'

'May it live to be a thousand. OK, now, tails aside, tell me the news!'

'The plans of the Guardians of Good Luck are much more devious and sinister than you might think.'

I pricked my ears at this. Cheapskate had my complete attention.

Faraway, we could hear the song of a drunken sailor. He sang a melancholy song about a heartless mermaid, who bewitched a dark-eyed sailor boy and took him to the deep bottom of the sea with her.

'What do you mean?' I asked.

'You'll freak out, man! The Guardians' conspiracy has not one but *three* stages. The first stage, as you already know, will be completed with the extermination of the last black cat on the island.'

'You mean yours truly.'

'Precisely. But this is not the end of their plans. Oh, no, far from it.'

'Go on . . .'

'There are two more stages.'

'What happens at the next stage?'

'They are going to exterminate all grey cats and any cat that's got even a tiny speck of black on its coat.'

'Are you serious?'

'Of course I am. I'd never dream of joking about such a serious matter. May I never taste cream cheese again, if I'm lying to you.'

'And the third stage?'

'They're planning to annihilate all cats!'

'All of them?'

'With no exception! Colour notwithstanding!'

'Even white ones?'

'Those, too.'

'But how are they going to persuade people to accept such a preposterous thing?'

'They'll start the rumour that appearances can be deceptive.'

'What does that mean?'

'It means that white cats are in reality black cats that changed colour just to save their skins.'

'I don't believe you. You're making it all up.'

'Mouse's honour! May my whiskers drop off and be trampled on by a hippopotamus if I'm lying! Orlop the much-travelled happened to eavesdrop on a conversation between the captain of a ship and a high-ranking Guardian.'

'But why? Why would they do all this? Why would they want to wipe out the entire cat world? What meaning, what purpose, what reason could this have?'

'They all have their own particular reasons. The Guardians

do what they do out of superstition. The politicians do it because they've got vested interests. Others do it for the financial benefit.'

'What do you mean?'

'Well, here's how it is. First of all, it suits politicians. By blaming cats for the misfortunes that have befallen the island, they find a convenient excuse for their own failures and for all the things going wrong on this island. Who is going to probe too deeply into the government's mistakes, the scandals, bribery, misuse of funds and waste of public money, when they have got the perfect scape-cats? If things are going to the dogs, just blame the cats! This is why the persecution has to continue and expand to include cats of other colours. After all, if black cats have been exterminated and they still have problems, people will see through the deceit. They'll realise that there are other reasons for their plight and will want to lay the blame elsewhere. That is when our honourable leaders will point the finger at grey cats and then all other cats . . .'

'And then?'

'Then they'll hope to think of something else, find another way, start another persecution, blame someone else to divert people's attention. In the meantime, of course, they'll have made a fortune. But, this is not all, my friend. There are many other secret and unlawful stakes behind the actions of the Guardians of Good Luck.'

'What are you trying to say?'

'There are others in this game who wish to take advantage of both the Guardians and the politicians – for their own purposes.'

'Who are they? What are their purposes?'

'You won't believe me if I tell you.'

'Speak up! I'm listening. Don't keep me in suspense.'

Cheapskate remained thoughtful for a while. 'Follow me!' he said finally.

'Where?'

'To the docks nearby. I want to show you something.'

I had no choice but to follow him. We got out of the pile of Persian carpets and Cheapskate led the way to the west end of the wharf, where four ships were anchored in a line, one yellow and three grey. All of them were huge – they were four of the biggest ships I had ever laid eyes on.

'Do you see these?' he asked.

'Yes, I do. Why are you showing them to me?'

'Do you know what the cargo of the yellow ship is?'

'Spices?'

'No.'

'Mosquito nets?'

'No.'

'Cornflour?'

'No.'

'Maize?'

'Nope. You'll never guess! Come, see with your own eyes.

Follow me. Just be careful though that these three don't get wind of us.'

I noticed then three hefty sailors with black shirts and droopy moustaches who were guarding that very part of the port.

Cheapskate and I leapt noiselessly from the wharf on to a barge and then, jumping from boat to boat, we arrived at the yellow ship. We swiftly climbed up some thick ropes that were hanging from the deck-rail and peered into the hold from a half-open porthole. I could make out hundreds of wooden crates stacked high, with the initials MT printed on them.

'See?' asked Cheapskate. 'Can you see what the yellow ship is carrying?'

'What? Mashed turnips?'

'No!'

'Erm . . . melodious trumpets?'

'Melodious trumpets, indeed! It's not carrying anything like that, you numbskull.'

'What is it carrying, then?'

'Mousetraps.'

'Traps? For mice?'

'No, for rhinos!' he said, sarcastically. 'Of course they are for mice!'

What was Cheapskate driving at?

'That's the case as far as the yellow ship is concerned. Let's take the other three ships, now. Do you know what the three grey ships are packed with?'

'What?'

'Would you like me to show you?'

'No, no! *Tell* me! I'll believe you ... What are they packed with?'

'Mice. Hundreds, thousands, *millions* of mice! Especially bred to withstand all poisons.'

'You must be joking.'

'Not at all. The Guardians of Good Luck have gone into business with the commercial import–export group IMT, which specialises in Ingenious Mouse Traps, as their name advertises, and aim to import the mousetraps you have just seen to our island.'

I remembered Ernest and Edmund De La Dupe, the twin directors, with their tiny, shifty eyes and pear-shaped bellies, whom I had met at Guillaume De La Bogue's mansion and later, at the entrance of the former Society for the Protection of Animals. I was slowly beginning to understand. At least, I now knew what the initials IMT stood for.

'Go on!' I encouraged him.

'When their plans have borne fruit and the entire cat population has been wiped off the face of the earth, when there isn't even *one* cat on the island, just for show, IMT's thugs intend to turn loose all these mice, millions of them, to flood the island.'

'Why on earth should they do that?' I queried.

'To sell those mousetraps at an exorbitant price.'

'No! It can't be so!'

'Oh, yes. It can very well be so. They're also planning to take advantage of the hurricane season, when no other ship can come close to the island, so that they can have the monopoly. That's exactly how it is, my friend. Prices will soar. Mousetraps will be selling like hot cakes! They're going to be worth their weight in gold to the panic-stricken islanders, whose houses will be invaded by mice. They'll become filthy rich. They're going to make a whopping fortune out of mousetraps.'

'You mean to say that they are systematically dispatching the cats of the island in order to make a profit by selling traps?'

'Precisely! Spot on! This is why, no doubt, all the Guardians have invested considerable sums of money in IMT shares.'

I was speechless, trying hard to digest the size of the conspiracy.

We heard the siren of a ship go off as it was getting into the port. Soon the wharf would be swarming with sailors.

'Why are you telling me all this?' I asked. 'Why are you standing by me? Why are you helping me? You're a mouse, are you not?'

'So what?'

'You should be happy that cats are going to be wiped out, shouldn't you?'

'Let me put it this way. If I am to leave this vain little world, I'd rather owe it to a cat than a mousetrap. Cats, at least, have a soul. When they seize you, they might have just had their dinner and decide against eating you; they might take pity on you and let you go; you might even become friends with you, just like us, now that I think about it. There's no chance with a trap. Have you ever seen a trap that couldn't manage another mouthful? Ever seen a friendly trap? Have you ever seen a trap with *feelings*?'

I could see the point he was trying to make. I thanked him for his help, took one last look at the great ships with their dreadful cargoes and, with a heavy heart, I went back to my hiding place, the pile of Persian rugs.

30

From bad to worse

In which the persecution spreads wider and all the cats on the island are exterminated in a most atrocious way.

Things progressed exactly as Cheapskate had predicted. Only the following morning, I heard the newspaper-sellers cry out, 'Special editiooool! Grey cats and cats with the slightest suspicion of black on their fur are outlawed! Special editiooool! Beware of treacherous grey cats! Special editiooool!'

Over the next days, the persecution of black cats was closely followed by the persecution of grey cats and then of cats of all other colours, including white. And sure enough, the new persecutions were just as cruel and efficient as the first.

Demonstrations were rife. The slogans were more or less familiar. I noticed that the demonstrators were using the same placards and the same banners, only they had crossed out the word 'black'. So, now they were saying . . .

STOP THE JINX TODAY
BUMP OFF A STRAY!

ENOUGH OF THE EVIL EYE
ALL CATS DESERVE TO DIE!

It was the same with posters. They were almost exactly the same as the originals, except for the word 'black' . . .

TO GET A CAT
USE A BASEBALL BAT!

IT IS EVERY PUPIL'S OBLIGATION
TO RAT ON A CAT
AND SAVE THE NATION.

Now that there was a precedent, people did not have the slightest compunction in denouncing, trapping or exterminating cats. They used any trick, any means, any manner. They used slings, shotguns, snares, stones, nets, traps and poisoned bait.

You saw stooping grandads clubbing cats with their walking sticks. You saw ten-year-olds aiming at cats with their slings. You saw elegant young ladies thumping cats on the head with dainty pink parasols. You saw high-society ladies letting their yapping Pekinese loose on cats. You saw old women on street corners, with bent backs and head-scarves, selling sachets of the most horrible cat poisons. At the crack of dawn, huntsmen climbed on rooftops and lay in wait with their shotguns and, at night, patrols with specially trained wolfhounds roamed the streets and alleys. At fairs, brawny wrestlers performed a variety of horrid stunts that involved cats to entertain the crowds. They grabbed them by the tail, spun them over their heads and competed against one another as to who would fling his cat the furthest.

There was a fairground where you could practise shooting live cats, hanging by their whiskers. If you got them, you won a chain of paper daisies or a pot of crimson nail varnish. At the same place, you could test your strength by pounding a hammer on a tin box that contained a cat. What's more, it was all the rage for children who played football to use tightly bound cats instead of balls.

Only but a few people resisted, expressed their objection or attempted to protest, and those who did were accused of catophilia. Considered a menace to society, they found themselves in deep trouble. They were defamed, their children were sent to asylums, their houses were pillaged and their property confiscated. Some catophiles were lynched. A priest who dared to condemn cat killers from the pulpit was accused of some sort of scandal and was defrocked. Even those who did not believe at all that cats are dangerous – those who knew only too well that other people were responsible for the country's misfortunes – decided to lie low and never said a word.

Cat-killers had become national heroes. Everybody chased cats. They tried to dig out, close in on, cheat, torture and exterminate cats. Some did it out of a sense of duty, some out of boredom, some out of fear and some out of sadistic pleasure. Yes, it's true! Some were having a ball doing it!

For example, a shop owner advertised his washing machines in the shop window by squeezing kittens into the drum. Crowds gathered to watch the tiny kittens spin in the washing machine for a laugh. There were others, at central squares, who flogged cats with a cat-o-nine-tails and then dropped their bodies into cauldrons filled with boiling water.

In some areas, the local authorities covered whole streets with glue. The unfortunate creatures that tried to cross the street to avoid their persecutors got stuck on the spot and were forced to watch – to their horror – as huge road-rollers, driven by teenage PCY (Proud Catocidal Youth) volunteers, moved slowly towards them, before they were squashed to a pulp.

There were some shrewd people who spread fish glue on to the street. When the hungry cats went to lick it, their tongues got stuck and they were caught.

In a few short weeks, there was not a cat to be seen at all.

31

A fire in the pigeon soft

In which our hero finds out who the traitor was that had informed the Guardians of Good Luck of the meeting on the coal shed.

One day, as I was chasing after a praying mantis on the rails of a disused train station, I heard a rustle in the tall grass and saw a white cat appear from behind it.

He was a sorry sight. Exhausted, muddy, with gummy eyes, a swollen muzzle and his fur matted all over his skinny ribs. One of his hind paws was crippled and he dragged it, uselessly, behind him. Round his neck hung the torn remains of a shiny silver ribbon.

'Save me! They're after me!' he muttered, out of breath.

Although he was dirty and moulted, a far cry from what he had looked like when I had first met him, I recognised him immediately. 'Rasmin!' I meowed in surprise. 'Is that you?'

'You know who I am?' he asked, baffled. 'Have we met before?'

'What does it matter, now? Follow me!'

I led him to my hiding place – the pigeon loft – and helped him hide. He was shaking with fear. His bleary eyes looked at me with gratitude, as if I were his last hope. There was no sign of that stuck-up cat who used to eat nothing but purée of boiled goldfish. There was no sign of his old splendour. He was a pitiful sight, now. His once sleek and shiny coat was dull and slimey, his tail was twisted out of shape, his ears scratched, scabby and purulent. I remembered the swanky cat furdresser with the apricot-coloured waistcoat, the purple neck scarf and the tight white linen trousers.

'Say, whatever happened to the cat furdresser?' I asked.

'He changed job. He has now become a dog-groomer. He specialises in Pekinese dogs. He got married to the maid with the ginger hair.'

'And . . .' I hesitated. 'And what about Graziella? What has become of her?'

Rasmin remained silent. Hadn't he heard my question or was there a reason why he hesitated to answer?

'Tell me! What has become of Graziella?' I insisted. 'I need to know.'

'The gardener turned her in.'

I remembered the gardener who had sprinkled the rose-bushes with rosewater and kicked me with his big, thick shoe.

'And then?'

'A gang of teenage thugs came and took her away. She suffered horribly at their hands.'

'What did they do to her?'

'They drowned her in a barrel of . . .'

'Of what?'

'Hot tar. One of the young louts came up with the idea of turning her into a zebra first. They painted black tar stripes on her coat. Then they threw her into the tar barrel. They laughed and jeered as she was burning and drowning.'

I shivered all over. My head was spinning. I couldn't stand listening to any more of this. 'Enough,' I said. 'How did *you* manage to get out of it?'

'I fainted. They thought I was dead and threw me into a rubbish pit. I've been a fugitive since then. I've just escaped some housewives who tried to hang me by the tail from the clothes line.' He stopped suddenly. 'Did you hear that? They're coming! We're doomed!'

'It's all right. It's only your imagination.' I calmed him down. 'I'll hide you. I'll help you in any way I can.'

'Do you really mean it?'

'Yes, Rasmin, I do.'

'But . . . where have we met? How do you know my name?'

I explained who I was. He was about to say something, then he stopped, as if thinking better of it. Finally, he decided to speak. 'Wait a minute,' he said. 'I must tell you something. I owe it to you.'

'What is it?'

'Do you remember the carnage at the coal shed?'

'How can I possibly forget it?'

'I –'

'What?'

'I betrayed you.'

'*You?*'

'Yes. I led them there. Graziella had told me about your meeting.'

'But *why*? How could you . . . Why?'

'I feared that Graziella would not forget all about you that easily.'

I said nothing. What could I have said, anyway? He was looking at me: frightened, repentant, pathetic. He wasn't the same cat that had betrayed us. He was someone else now. A pitiful shadow of his former self. What point was there in my feeling spiteful against him?

'I'm hungry!' he meowed. 'You don't happen to have a spare goldfish?'

I remembered the scene at the greenhouse, the dainty porcelain plate with the gilt initials. I felt like laughing. 'No, no goldfish, I'm afraid, but we'll find something! Wait here for me.'

I went down to the river, hopped on to a rock, lay in wait for a while and before long, managed to catch two minnows. I ate one and took the other in my mouth to give to Rasmin.

As I approached I could hear voices. I peered from behind some gooseberry bushes. A round-faced boy with light brown hair was talking animatedly to a broad-shouldered patrolman of the Emergency Cat Extermination Squad who was carrying a huge spiky club.

'Are you sure you saw them round here?' asked the cat patrolman.

'Yes.'

'Where exactly?'

'There! Near the pigeon loft.'

They had spotted us. It was best that I vanished so they would lose my tracks. Silently, I buried myself in the wood and let a couple of hours go by. Then I took the way back to the pigeon loft. The first sign that something was wrong was the smell that hit my nose. A smell of burnt wood.

Then I saw the smoke and the debris. They had set fire to the pigeon loft. My hiding place had turned to ashes. In the background I could make out a patrol with armbands and helmets marching out. There was no sign of Rasmin. Perhaps he had managed to get away. Perhaps he had been caught. Perhaps – and most likely – he had been burnt alive.

I didn't feel like eating the other fish. I lay it on the smouldering ashes of the torched pigeon loft and went away with my head bent.

The following day, I heard the special news bulletin on the portable radio of a group of hunters with pheasant feathers on their hats, who were having a picnic under the shadow of an oak tree.

'The last two fugitive cats met their just end,' rang the announcer's voice, triumphantly. 'They became prey to the flames in their hiding place, an old pigeon loft in an abandoned farmyard.'

So, everyone believed I'd burnt to death, I thought. That was good. That meant they wouldn't go after me any more.

Then the Prime Minister came on the air. 'Dear fellow citizens,' he began, and his voice trembled with excitement and patriotic fervour. 'This is the dawning of a new era for our island. A blessed time of happiness, blissfulness, merriment, affluence and prosperity. An age without worries, disappointments, hardships and adversity. An era when misfortune and bad luck are but a distant memory. A golden era, indeed. The government proudly proclaims this day a national holiday. The festivities, which will include spectacular fireworks, open-air concerts, folk dances and a plethora of spectacles for your entertainment, will commence this evening.'

The hunters applauded, threw their hats in the air and embraced one another, full of emotion. A well-built hunter with close-cropped hair and bushy eyebrows, who was drinking wine from a flask, threw it away, got hold of his shotgun and started to shoot in the air, overwhelmed with patriotic enthusiasm.

I waited for some time and when I saw the sun had begun to set, taking every possible precaution – a shadow among the shadows – I ventured a walk round the rooftops of the city.

In the brightly lit streets and in the squares, exhilarated crowds were celebrating in a frenzy of euphoria. Wild enthusiasm had taken over everyone. Young men and women danced in the central squares, children threw balloons and confetti from the balconies, grannies climbed lampposts and waved their headscarves, smiling clowns did somersaults and stood upside down on the pavements. And amidst the music and laughter, the cat-killers, cat patrolmen and cat torturers marched proudly, wearing shiny medals with horseshoes and four-leafed clovers.

When I had seen what I had come to see, I left the sounds of the revelry behind me and returned to the wood.

During the next days, I slept wherever I could lay my head, here and there, in ditches, under thick foliage, in the hollows of fallen trees. Every time I heard the footsteps of a woodcutter or a farm hand I hid in terror. At nights, I kept waking up from dreadful nightmares. I saw Choptail's body, covered in blood, tossed in the air by the spiked club; Tarmac writhe with pain on the blood-soaked sand of the playground; Purrcy startled by the kicks of the enraged coachman. I dreamed of Ebonina sinking into the lime pit, Graziella drowning in the barrel of hot tar, or

Rasmin struggling to escape the inferno of the burning pigeon loft. I would wake in terror, breathing hard, as if all the air around me had been sucked out.

Then there were times when I felt so sorry for myself, I plunged into the chaos of despair. My heart would almost burst with all the bitter memories. I would imagine that I grew bigger, wilder, gigantic; that I changed into a mighty tiger, a huge, avenging beast that would hunt down our executioners and tear them to shreds.

I wasn't a mighty tiger, though. I was just a cat. A plain, helpless cat . . . The last cat left alive on the island. This is why I thought I was hallucinating, that I'd lost my reason for good, when, one day, as I lay in wait in a wood with juniper bushes on the off chance I'd happen upon a grasshopper or a cricket, I heard that familiar song coming from far away, as if in a dream:

> *I knew a cat called Abigail*
> *Who had such a lovely tail . . .*

It couldn't be. I had to be hallucinating.

> *All the tom cats stood in line*
> *To date this divine feline.*
> *They got the deepest thrill*
> *From her tail's dainty frill.*

There they lay
To see it sway

I stood still. The song stopped. But then it continued. I could hear it crystal clear as it drew nearer and nearer . . .

You are pretty,
Lovely kitty,
So I sing this little ditty

Ah, I wish, my Abigail
You had more than just one tail!

The wet undergrowth quivered, parted and the muzzle of a cat appeared. It was a black, pitch black cat. I stood still as if I had been struck by thunder. Dear God in heaven! It was – Choptail!

32

Escape from hell

In which Choptail recounts his unbelievable adventure in the dark dungeons of a fur factory.

'Choptail,' I stammered. 'Is that you? Is that really you or is it your ghost?'

He looked as if he'd been through unbelievable hardship, but that old sparkle was still in his eyes, as always.

'It's me all right, you old beggar!' he retorted. 'Your friend, Choptail, the Sizzler, the Commandocat!'

I was over the moon with joy. There was so much I was dying to tell him, so many things I wanted to ask him.

'Where . . . how . . . what happened . . . How did you survive . . . How did you get here?'

'I escaped.'

'From where?'

'From hell.'

'What hell?'

'From the dungeons of Armand Rapacine's fur factory.'

The name rang a bell . . . I tried to place it.

'What happened exactly? Explain. Tell me everything! Every single thing!'

Choptail told me his story. 'When you left me at the coal shed, I wasn't dead as you had thought.'

'But I saw you pass away! I saw you with my own eyes . . .'

'Well, that was my eighth life.

'The eighth?'

'Yes, I've only got one left. That's why I should be extremely careful from now on. I can't take any more chances.'

'It must be true then, what some people say, that cats have nine lives.'

'But of course! I was exhausted, numb with pain, but not dead. I came to some time later, but the minute I tried to get out of the coal shed, I fell into the hands of the short man with the greasy cap – you know, the one who smelled of iodine and mint.'

'Yes, I know. Didn't the beast kill you? Didn't he drown you in the hamam of terror?'

'No, fortunately not. Shorty, you see, did not drown all cats he caught. He got the money from the other guy – the one with the white suit and the dark-green glasses – but kept two or three cats from each batch on the side and sold them secretly to Armand Rapacine. He was doing very nicely out of both sides!'

Armand Rapacine . . . The name reminded me of something, but what? Suddenly, I had a flash . . . I remembered the meeting at the park. I remembered the guy who was sitting on the bench that afternoon, talking to Shorty in a voice that sounded like a rotten apple plunging into the sewer. I remembered everything very clearly. I could see him now, counting the greasy banknotes, one by one, and hand them over to Shorty.

'What does this Armand Rapacine do?'

'He's a furrier! He runs a company called FFF – Fantastic Fleece and Furs.'

My own fur stood on end.

'He's got about seventy cats imprisoned in the cellars of his fur factory. He intends to turn them into –'

'What? Fur coats?'

'No. Flocats or flocatty as he calls them.'

'What's a flocatty when it's at home?'

'A flocat. A traditional fur rug made of cat fur.'

'You're pulling my leg!'

'No, not at all. He's even got his jingle ready:

> *'A traditional flocatty*
> *Never looks shabby or tatty*
> *It's the one you will adore*
> *Once you've put it on your floor.'*

I thought of myself as a 'flocatty' rug on the floor of a sitting room and an icy hand ran all over my spine.

'He's planning to make a fortune by selling them to collectors at astronomical prices. As you understand I'm sure, they will soon be collectors' items due to the distinct lack of cats on the island!' Choptail continued.

'You know what? This man you just mentioned – I met him earlier.'

'Where?'

I told him all about Rapacine's meeting with Shorty at the park. 'He said something about some dwarves,' I said. 'What did he mean?'

'He's got three dwarves working for him. They're flayers. They wear hoods to cover their faces and boots made of thick buffalo hide. Only their eyes show. They say they get a kick out of torturing cats and flay them alive. Rapacine allows them to do so because he believes that the quality of the fur improves this way. Come to think of it, we would all most probably have been flayed already if they didn't enjoy torturing us in one more way.'

'What is that?'

'They'd come down to the cellar every now and then and yelled, "This is it, pussies! The honeymoon is over! Now it's time for some serious flaying!" You can imagine our terror. But then they'd shake their heads and say, "Nah, we're not in prime shape today. We'll come back some other time." And they'd leave us there to sweat. They'd play this game every two or three days. And they are most probably doing the same now. I was lucky that I managed to escape.'

'How did you do it?'

'Fortunately, the lock on my cage had become rusty so I managed to get out of it and then I ran away, unnoticed. But enough about me. What about you? Tell me your story . . .'

I told him. We talked for hours. Then we snuggled into the cosy hollow of an old chestnut tree and fell asleep. I hadn't slept so peacefully in ages.

33

A daring plan

In which the two friends help Armande Rapacine's prisoners escape from the fur factory and then plan to sink a ship.

The following morning found us optimistic and ready for action. We breakfasted on some grasshoppers and there, under the old oak tree, I told Choptail everything I had learned from Cheapskate. I told him about the connections between IMT and the Guardians of Good Luck, about their plans and the four ships at the dock.

He listened attentively, while munching on a daisy. 'We're on a sticky wicket, here,' he remarked when I had finished. 'Stickier than the tree you got glued on! We must plan our moves carefully. If we're lucky – who knows? – we might manage to slip into a boat and leave this cursed island for ever.'

'I have no intention of leaving!' I declared sharply. I took him by surprise.

'What do you mean?'

'This is my island. This is where I was born, where I grew up and no one is going to drive me away! Besides, I get seasick . . .'

'Then what?'

'Listen, Choptail,' I said. 'Here's what I think we should do. First and foremost, we have to free the cats from the cellars of Armand Rapacine's fur factory.'

'I went through hell to get out of there and now you're asking me to go back?'

'If you haven't got the heart, after all you've been through, I understand. I'll go alone.'

'That's out of the question. Wherever you go, I go, too! Wherever you are, I'll be by your side!'

The tall grass swayed lazily in the light breeze. A blue butterfly sat on my friend's ear. He tried to snatch it but it flew away and landed on an anemone.

'Good,' I said. 'That's what I wanted to hear. But releasing all prisoner cats is not enough. We've got to do one more thing.'

'What is that?'

'A daring sabotage.'

'I like daring sabotages. Count me in. I love action. What have you got in mind?'

'We'll sink the yellow ship with the mousetraps.'

'Did I hear right? *We* will sink a whole *ship*? What do

you think a ship is? A paper boat?'

'We'll find a way. We have to sink it at the right moment, though. Not too soon nor too late. It has to be timed with precision.'

'And what is the right moment, pray?'

'As soon as the conspirators let the mice loose from the grey ships and before they have had time to unload the mousetraps from the yellow one! What do you say? Reckon we can pull it off?'

'Why not? As long as we know their plans to the last detail.'

'There's only one way to find out,' I said and jumped up. 'Follow me!'

'Where to?'

'To the port.'

'Now?'

'We haven't got time to waste. We're a long way from the sea and we'll have to change our route and hide all the time to escape detection. I reckon it will be dark by the time we get there.'

'All right, if you insist – let's go!'

We set off straightaway. We went through woods, prairies and spinneys, avoiding the open ground and many uneventful hours later, we arrived at the port. We crept along the wharf, hid behind some sacks of aromatic jasmine tea and kept our ears pricked. As the sailors from the four big ships strolled by, we listened to their conversations and picked up the important facts – the mice were due to be released from the three grey ships on Saturday night. The mousetraps would be unloaded at the crack of dawn on Monday morning and then distributed to the shops.

'Listen carefully, Choptail,' I said. 'Tomorrow we'll release the cats from the fur factory. On Saturday, as soon as they have let the mice loose, we'll sink the yellow ship. Let's see how our persecutors manage to pull through without mousetraps and without cats.'

'Done,' said Choptail, who was beginning to pick up enthusiasm. 'Let's get to it!'

34

The prisoners of the fur factory

*In which the escape from the cellars of the fur factory
goes according to plan, until the sudden appearance
of Armand Rapacine and the three flayers.*

In order to free the imprisoned cats from the fur factory, we
decided to call on Mother Reene for help. We found her
behind the granaries, in a makeshift shed made of old planks
and sheet-irons that had a patchwork rug for a door. We
explained the situation in detail and she immediately agreed
to help us, without a second thought.

The following morning, she put on her best clothes, did
her hair and face and went to the fur factory. Fortunately, she
succeeded in persuading Rapacine to employ her as a cleaner
for ridiculously low wages.

She found out the whereabouts of the cats, got the
bunch of keys to the dungeon and the cages, and, that very
evening, as soon as the furrier, the accountant and the rest of

the staff had gone home, she opened the door for us.

Cautiously, we went down to the dreary, badly lit cellars of the fur factory and there we met a sight that I will never forget as long as I live. There was row upon row of cages with imprisoned cats. They were frightened, silent, resigned to their fate, their eyes full of despair.

'Your torment is over! We've come to save you!' I cried, while Mother Reene, without wasting time, started to open the cages one by one and set the cats free.

You can imagine their joy! Festive meowing and purrs of gratitude sounded all around. Among them, I heard a familiar mewing. My heart missed a beat. It was as if I could hear Ebonina. But surely it was some other cat with a voice that sounded like hers. I moved closer to the spot the mewing had come from and peered through the dim light of the damp basement. What I saw brought a thousand memories flooding back . . . The same sleek, black coat, the same graceful tail, the same luminous blue eyes. There was no doubt. It *was* her. My Ebonina. I looked at her in silence, as if time had stopped. So did she.

'I thought you were gone for ever,' I managed to say, touching her tentatively. 'An old tortoise told me she had seen you jump into the lime pit.'

'Yes, I did jump, actually, but –'

'But what?'

'I was lucky. I landed on a plank that had slipped into the

pit and was floating, half-covered with lime. One dip of my paw into the white liquid and I figured out what was going on. When the wind blew the plank near the bank, I jumped – it was the hardest jump of my life, but I made it.'

'And then?'

'I hadn't managed to get very far, when I walked straight into a patrol of Guardians. They nabbed me and I ended up here, in this horrible dungeon.'

She showed me her tiny front paw. The lime burn still hadn't healed. I felt as if she had been returned to me from the next world.

In the meantime, Mother Reene had finished opening the remaining cages. I explained to my fellow cats that we had to get out of the fur factory without being detected, as soon as possible, and head for an abandoned circus that I had spotted earlier on and hide in there until further notice.

'When we get out in the street, make sure you keep your eyes closed because their shine might betray our presence!' added Choptail. 'Use your sense of smell instead!'

At the front of the line there was Mother Reene, then me, with Choptail and Ebonina and the rest of the cats behind them. Among them were Lara and her kitten, reunited. We crept up the dank stairs that led out of the cellars, went through two underground doors and emerged in a long corridor paved with white tiles, which was dimly lit by a dusty naked lightbulb. Left and right we could see two rows of closed doors with tortoiseshell handles. One of the doors said 'Flaying Preparation Room', another bore the words 'Flaying Room' while the third had a sign which said 'Torture Chamber For Half-flayed Cats'.

As we moved on, we heard the front door open with a blood-curdling screech. We froze in our tracks! Mother Reene stopped, holding her breath and so did we. I saw the ominous silhouette of Armand Rapacine loom at the door. The lights went on. He was flabby with pink cheeks and protruding eyes the colour of rotting cabbage and three fat chins. He was wearing a mink hat, a bearskin coat with a rabbit-fur collar, buckskin shoes and crocodile-leather gloves with a matching watch strap. Three dwarves with moleskin hoods and buffalo-leather boots followed at his heel. You couldn't see their faces as they were completely covered by hoods but their devilish eyes shone piercingly in the dark. They must have been the flayers.

Rapacine saw that the light of the corridor was on and must have suspected that there was something going on. He paused for a while, as if thinking. Then he walked decisively in our direction. If he turned the corner we were doomed. He'd see us for sure, he would establish what had happened and sooner or later we would all end up in one of the three rooms.

It was then that Mother Reene did something bold that I will remember for as long as I live. She went round the bend of the corridor and stood in front of Rapacine, blocking his way. 'Good evening, your excellency, Monsieur Rapacine,' she said courteously.

The furrier had not expected to see her. He seemed taken by surprise but immediately recovered and fixed a cold accusing stare at the old lady.

'Who are you, woman?'

'The new cleaner, sir,' replied brave Mother Reene. 'Don't you remember, sir? You hired me only this morning.'

He eyed her from top to bottom, suspiciously, beginning to recognise her. 'What are you still doing here?'

'I was cleaning . . .'

'At this hour?'

'Yes.'

'Why?'

'Erm . . . I thought I might . . . because it was so dusty . . .' Mother Reene faltered. 'It's a wicked thing, dust is.'

I could feel the suspicion grow in Rapacine's steely eyes. It was obvious he did not believe a word. 'What kind of fool do you take me for, woman? Do you think I buy all this?' He lifted his hand and wagged a sausage-like finger in front of Mother Reene's face. 'Confess! You've come here to steal, haven't you?'

'No!'

'Why are you here, then?'

'To . . . to . . .'

My heart was beating fast. All the other cats stood still, as if they had been embalmed, waiting for the fateful reply. Would she snitch on us, to save herself?

'Yes . . . I came here to steal!' muttered Mother Reene. 'May God forgive me. I was in terrible need . . .'

She was admitting to being a thief to save us from the flayers!

'I should have expected that,' barked Rapacine. 'It's my fault for taking pity on you, for trusting you and giving you a job to feed yourself. Follow me, you thieving old cow! I'll call the police! They'll put you in the nick and that'll teach you to take advantage of honest, god-fearing furriers like myself. Come with me, too.' He beckoned to the flayers. 'Just make sure she doesn't run for it. They're crafty, those old hags.'

Armand Rapacine turned on his heel and went into an office a bit further back, on his right. Mother Reene and the dwarves followed him. The entrance door was still open. I signalled to the other cats and we slipped noiselessly out into the darkness of the welcoming night.

If an inhabitant of the island had happened to look out of his window that night, he would have seen a litany of black cats silently making their way in the dark, heading for the abandoned circus. But, luckily for us, no one did.

35

The Yellow Ship

In which our hero finds a way to sink a ship.

'The first part of the plan went like clockwork!' declared Choptail after we had all arrived safe and sound at our temporary refuge.

Having left the other cats behind to get some rest, Choptail, Ebonina and myself were sitting at one of the inside yards of the circus, on a canon mounted on a blue base that was once used for the cannonball man's act.

'What are the police going to do to Mother Reene?' I asked Choptail anxiously.

'Don't worry. She's not in any real danger. After they've found out that she hasn't actually stolen anything, she'll get away with a warning at the most. She'll lose her job, of course, but she didn't want it anyway. She only got it to help us.'

'Good. Then all that's left is to sink the yellow ship,' I said. 'I don't think it will be that much of a problem.'

'*Excusez-moi* for not sharing your optimism,' Choptail cut in, 'but, believe me, sinking a great big ship is no walk in the park!'

'Oh, come on.'

'No, tell me – have you ever sunk a ship?'

'No.'

'A sailing boat?'

'No.'

'A dinghy?'

'No.'

'So what exactly do you think a ship is, then? A bathtub, and all we'll have to do is pull the plug?'

'It won't be that easy, is that what you're saying?'

'Not at all. It will be almost impossible.'

'If we gnawed at the cables that tie it to the wharf?' suggested Ebonina, who had been filled in on the details.

'It wouldn't sink. It would drift away at the most and they would probably catch up with it.'

'Right,' remarked Choptail. 'If we want the ship to sink to the bottom we have to bore holes in it somehow.'

'But how? And with what?'

'With – with –'

'With what?'

'With our claws?' I suggested.

'No way. Have you ever managed to bore a hole in a piece of wood with your claws?'

I had to admit that I hadn't even attempted to do such a thing. The three of us remained thoughtful for quite a while.

'Holes! Holes . . . How on earth could we bore holes in a ship?' I wondered.

The moon sailed on its course across the sky. An acrobat doing a balancing act was looking at us from a half-torn poster, stuck on a mossy circus wagon. In the distance we could hear the hooting of an owl.

'I've got it!' I meowed suddenly. 'I know what we'll do!'

'What?'

'We'll call for reinforcements!'

'What do you mean?'

'I know someone who specialises in holes!'

I left Choptail and Ebonina behind, waiting with puzzled expressions on their muzzles and, quick as lightning, like a straight arrow, I ran to the wood with the lovesick wood-peckers. Day was breaking as I arrived. It didn't take long to find Wallace and he was very happy to see me.

'Can I help you in any way, my dear friend?' he asked.

'Perhaps you could.'

'I am all ears.'

I climbed the walnut tree with the twelve hearts carved into its trunk. 'It is about a ship.'

'Where is it?'

'At the port. Do you think you could make a few holes in it?'

'But if I make holes in it, my good friend, it will flood with water and sink!'

'That's exactly what I'm after!'

'Why?'

'I've got my reasons.'

'Couldn't you tell me?'

'I'll explain another time. What I need to know now is, can you do it or not?'

'But of course I can. It is but a piece of seedcake! Boring holes is what I specialise in!' Wallace assured me.

'Say . . . could you manage to do it secretly, in just one night?'

'No, that is out of the question!'

'Oh. That's a pity . . .'

'Hold on! What I meant is, that it is out of the question that I'll manage on my own! However, if I mobilise all the woodpeckers in the wood, we'll turn your little ship into a sieve before you can say "buttonhole".'

'You rule! I knew I could depend on you! It's official, then. See you tomorrow night at the wharf.'

I gave Wallace detailed instructions and was about to return to the circus, but my footsteps led me elsewhere . . . I went to the wood with the chestnut trees, where I had followed Ebonina on her fateful appointment. I looked for the spot where she had met the gang. When I arrived at the tree, I found it burnt almost to the ground by lightning.

There was no sign of Knups, Lily or Isabella.

When I looked at the grass, though, among the wild flowers and the mushrooms I caught a glimpse of something shiny. I moved closer and saw that it was Ebonina's rose-coloured ribbon with the silver bell, only it was now tarnished and covered in mud. I thought I might give it a wash in the nearby brook and take it to my darling. But then I changed my mind. It would be best if I didn't remind her of those moments. I buried the silver bell in the ground, covered it with soil and grass and returned to our hiding place.

When I told the others the news about the woodpeckers, they could hardly contain their eagerness and enthusiasm.

On Saturday night, Choptail, Wallace and I hid on the roof of the pub The Whining Herring, near the west wharf. We saw a dozen men from IMT approaching. They were wearing tall black hats and had droopy moustaches. They went on board the three grey ships and let the mice loose. A swirling tide of millions of rodents gushed like a grey torrent out of the holds of the ships, spread across the quayside and flooded the sleepy streets like live rivers. The whole island would soon be thick with them.

In the meantime, the woodpecker workforce, some two hundred birds in total, divided into smaller groups to avoid raising any suspicions, were lined up under penthouses, on masts, bulwarks, cranes and the wires of the port, even on the cables of the ships and various other key points, poised for action.

'Fine!' I said as soon as the men from IMT had gone. 'I now proclaim the beginning of Operation Colander. Wallace, as soon as I have taken care of the guard, be prepared to give the signal to your team to start work.'

The guard, a scowling type with bushy eyebrows, long side whiskers and a big, square jaw, was my personal charge. A hole would do for him, too. He sat unsuspectingly on a bollard on the pier and smoked his pipe, lost in his daydreams. I approached carefully and peed all over his right trouser leg. I would be lying if I said that I didn't enjoy it. As soon as he felt the moisture seep through, he let out a yell, jumped up, saw me, put two and two together and started to chase after me, swearing loudly all the time. I lured him straight into a dark alley, where earlier I had spotted an uncovered manhole that led to the sewer, with the grid lying on the side. With a well-judged leap I flew over the hole, while he, as I had expected, fell right into it. That was one down, then! He was sewerly out of the way!

When I returned to the wharf, Wallace and his gang had already found their way into the holds of the yellow ship through the open portholes and had started working, while a group of cats, with Ebonina at the head, was methodically cutting the cables that held the ship tied to the pier with their teeth.

The following morning, the island was flooded with hundreds, thousands, millions of hungry grey mice. The yellow ship with its priceless load of mousetraps had vanished.

36

Panic on the island

*In which the island becomes infested with mice and
the islanders have no means to deal with them.*

To wake up at the crack of dawn to find you're
surrounded by about a dozen hefty mice, which are
playing volleyball on your bed with the half-eaten pompon
of your slipper, or are dancing the boogie round the night
lamp on your bedside table, or are munching pieces of
cheese, leaning happily on your alarm clock, is not a
particularly pleasant experience if you happen to be human.

The island was infested with mice and, because there
were no cats or mousetraps, the islanders had no way of
getting rid of them.

Shrill cries sounded everywhere that morning. You could
see mice performing at the clothesline as if it were at the
horizontal bar. There were mice dancing the Charleston on
window ledges, mice turning double-flip dives into tureens
of fish soup, mice scampering up traffic policemen's trousers

and snatching cheese pies from street vendors before running away.

Wave upon wave of mice flowed up the streets, engulfed the pavements, swarmed up walls and hedges, flooded terraces, backyards, rooftops and alleys.

Two ships laden with mousetraps that attempted to reach the island did not make it through the hurricanes. Word had it, they had both sunk.

On the island, uncontrollable panic prevailed and it grew with every passing hour. There were demonstrations, protests, accusations, charges, marches! A resourceful reporter discovered evidence of the conspiracy hatched by the Guardians of Good Luck, their dealings with the government and the financial interests of IMT. The following day, newspapers declared in bold titles:

SHAME!
CON MEN EXTERMINATE CATS
AND INFEST THE ISLAND
WITH MICE!

MICE MULTIPLY UNCONTROLLABLY!

EPIDEMICS NEXT?

MICE RULE!

NOT A SINGLE CAT
TO HUNT THEM DOWN!

Some ministers resigned. Some went on trial. One committed suicide. The government fell. Those that were held accountable were sent to prison. The rest either gave themselves up or hid in basements, attics, caves or in a certain steam bath . . .

Now it was the right moment to make an appearance, I reckoned.

When we marched triumphantly into the central square of the island, myself leading the procession, followed by seventy-five cats, we received a hero's welcome. They applauded us, they fed us, they petted us, they took pride in us, they fawned upon us. In a few hours we had sent the mice into a disorderly retreat. They daren't show their whiskers any more.

So, this is how cats were saved. This is how IMT went under. This is how I became a hero.

Epilogue

It didn't take long for our island to fall back into its old routine. Cats multiplied. Fear vanished, together with mistrust. It was as if the great persecution, that horrible injustice, had never happened.

Everything is peaceful now. People behave in their usual way. Some adore us, some dislike us, some feed us, some ignore us. We get a kick in the ribs now and then.

All those who were bent on annihilating us go to work in the morning, do their shopping, celebrate their birthday, take their children for a walk in the square. I even heard that Shorty convinced those in charge that he had repented and was voted vice president of the new Society for the Protection of Animals.

Have I lost my faith in human beings? you may ask. How could I, when for every Guillaume De La Bogue and Armand Rapacine there is one Marilena and one Mother Reene and who knows how many more?

Every once in a while, I go to Peter Pentameter the poet's

house and have a chat with Cheapskate, who was cornered by a few cats in the great panic, but was saved thanks to my prompt intervention and is now living happily ever after.

Sometimes, I think of the unjust death of my mate Tarmac. Do you think he's got a life left in him, like Choptail? Is there a chance I might come across him one day, round the bend of a remote street? Do you think so? Well, who knows, eh?

I'm standing now on the tin roof of the shed where my adventure started, looking at the fish tavern, the infinite sea, the dirt road, the passers-by. I can see groups of kids kicking rag-balls and licking strawberry ice creams greedily, young couples walking hand in hand, white-haired grannies pushing baby prams . . . From time to time, I sneak a look at the yard below and see Ebonina, lying among the mallows and the camomile, feeding our seven ebony kittens.

Everything is so quiet, so tranquil, so peaceful . . .

How can all this have happened? I wonder and try to convince myself that never, ever, will something like this happen again.

Deep down in my heart, though, I know that here, on our island, like anywhere else, cats forget, people forget, and it won't take much for the madness to begin all over again . . .